Dear Reside
I hope yo
Good Luc

Resident
June 2022

♡ Brandi

Leigh

Pretty Evil

PRETTY EVIL

Confessions of a Demon Hunter
~1~

BRANDI LEIGH

Cover artwork by
Moonstruck Cover Design & Photography
https://moonstruckcoverdesign.com

Edited by Margo Dill
https://www.editor-911.com

DEDICATION

For my kids, follow your dreams and always do what you love.

ACKNOWLEDGMENTS

To my tribe, I couldn't do this without you—
especially my Lit Ladies:
Margo, Tricia, Sarah, Grace, and Camille.

A special thank you to my mom, sisters, and the rest
of my family and friends.

PROLOGUE

St. Louis Cathedral, New Orleans, Louisiana
Confession

Father Peter Benz, Chancellor of St. Michael's Institute of Exorcism and Spiritual Warfare, and commonly known as Father Pete, stepped into the confessional, taking a seat in the wooden chair, which sat sideways to the screen.

He flipped a switch to the green light on the outside of his confessional to signal that he was ready. Lavive opened the narrow, wooden door, taking the position on the kneeler covered by a thin, maroon cushion; she faced the screen between them.

After a few moments, Lavive began, "Forgive me, Father, for I have sinned. It's been three days since my last confession, but three months since I've been here." The old kneeler creaked, as she fidgeted.

Father Pete adjusted the purple stole draped over his shoulders.

Lavive sighed. "Who knew one week could hold all the sins? Lies, coveting, cursing, and even

I

murder?" she said matter-of-factly.

Father Pete straightened in his seat. He leaned toward the screen.

"Let me be clear," she said, her voice soft but determined. "I didn't kill anyone. But yes, many people died."

Father Pete rubbed his jaw.

"I will tell you what. Fighting the Devil is a damn hard job." Lavive wrung her hands together.

Father Pete turned to look at her, seeing only a hazy silhouette of Lavive and her long, white dreadlocks perched on top of her head. "Why do I do this?" She balled her fists and gritted her teeth.

"Lavive, only you can answer that question."

"That is a very priest-like response," she said, rubbing her temples. "I know you are a priest first. But seriously, I need your advice, as my mentor, Father Pete." Her voice cracked a little.

"I understand." He paused. "You have been gifted and with that, comes the call to action. Some of us are called to the religious life, others to consecrated life, and still others, like you, called to something dangerous. But the Lord is always with you; you can always count on that."

"I know, Father Pete, I know." She sighed and put her elbows on the ledge of the screen.

"Do you want to continue?" he asked.

"Yes." She cleared her throat. "I have a flight in a couple of hours; we are heading to Las Vegas," she said and rolled her shoulders.

"We?" Father asked

"Yeah, we."

"Okay, we'll get to that in a moment. Let's begin again. Tell me more about the situation that opened you up to all these sins."

"Well, it all started in Chicago. I was chasing a chaos demon; that one was really slippery."

"Yes, I remember the call from the Diocese of Chicago, asking for help with the events happening around the city."

"Yeah, well, it ended up being smarter than I gave it credit. I tracked it for a few months, and I couldn't get close enough. I was really beginning to doubt my hunting instincts. I was a few blocks away when the shooting started—"

ONE

My feet hit the pavement seemingly in sync with the flashing red and white lights. Hundreds of survivors milled around, stunned, as the police tried to keep some form of order. The wounded were treated in a triage area, where ambulances lined up, making a semicircle in the superstore parking lot. White sheets covered the dead in a row too long for me to count. With the hundreds of people gathered, there were hundreds of angels floating just above, all in prayer.

They were all at least ten-feet tall with iridescent-lighted bodies and large, expansive wings. Each angel was similar but slightly different, all with large, masculine bodies and soft, feminine faces — ever stoic, never showing any emotion. I took a moment to relish in the beauty of them. Like an ocean of dancing light rolling just above the human devastation, I thanked God for this gift of sight.

I had searched day and night to find and prevent events like this. I had missed tracking this chaos demon by mere minutes, although it had actually begun its wrath a few weeks earlier with an apartment fire on the north side of Chicago.

I knew more about demons than the average twenty-five year old. I'd studied at St. Michael's Institute of Exorcism and Spiritual Warfare, focusing on deliverance and demonology for the past five years and honing my gifts of the Spirit.

"How many wounded?" I asked an EMT who was wrapping a gunshot wound on an older black man's arm. Out of the corner of my eye, I saw the black man's angel floating above him. The angel's arms were outstretched, his hands open as thin rays of light flowed from its palms. The light rained down upon the man, like a spring shower made of the purest love. It was beautiful and showed how each angel tried to assist the wards, even if there was free will. They still had a job, and this angel's job had a gunshot wound.

"I don't know; they keep coming." The EMT's gaze lingered a moment on my face and hair; I held my breath. I always got looks. There weren't many multi-mixed females, with African, Caucasian, and

Japanese cultures, running around with white dreadlocks and sapphire blue eyes. I was born to stand out, which was a cosmic joke, considering all I needed to do was hide.

He turned back to the injured man, and I relaxed, grateful he didn't notice my fake Chicago PD uniform.

I'd found over the years of chasing demons that it's a lot easier to dress the part of a cop than to be a spectator. No one noticed my fake uniform in the chaos of the events, especially the mass shooting. I wasn't there to make any waves; I was just doing my job, searching for that damn chaos demon that had started this mess and cast it back to Hell.

Walking a few feet away from the EMT, I re-centered and closed my eyes, saying a quick prayer to St. Michael, the true badass archangel. I wasn't an archangel or an angel for that matter.

When I went through confirmation in the Catholic Church at age 18, I received the charisms of divine sight, tongues, intercessory prayer for healing, and discernment of spirits. It didn't happen all at once; first, I had seen angels and demons, which led me to find Father Pete and St. Michael's Institute of Exorcism and Spiritual Warfare. I had thought I was the one possessed! After learning more about the gifts I was given, I wasn't sure how to use them. But since my training at the institute, I had come to know that I was a demon hunter. I'd been so good at hunting demons, the best, that the demons gave me a nickname--The Deliverer! I didn't mind the title; it gave me a little clout with the fallen. When dealing with the Devil, I needed all the help I could get.

After the prayer to St. Michael, I saw the chaos demon I'd been hunting. The demon smoke, not the smoke of a fire or anything earthly, was my sign. It was the smoke of the damned — a semi-solid ribbon of evil, twisting and curving around the people's legs. I took off in a full run toward the smoke. I wound through the people, chasing the thickening ribbon. Not all demons left a trail, but one that just set off a major mass shooting and pure chaos left a trail, which was great for me, the hunter.

I had to get it this time. I'd missed this chaos demon last month when it had struck the northern part Chicago in that fire. The apartment complex had been burned to the ground, leaving two dead and fourteen injured. Not a huge body count for a demon of this hierarchy — that's how I knew it'd strike again. It would want more. The tool of hate the demon used changed this time from fire to gun, but the result was always the same — death and fear.

My stomach tightened, as I passed a line of covered bodies; they came in all sizes, but the little ones got to me. I should have stopped this a month ago. I should have been better…faster…anything; but here I was, among the dead and dying, chasing the trail.

"I will get you," I said to myself, following the fattened ribbon of smoke. The smell of sulfur and the hair on my neck standing on end reassured me I was on the right track. Leaping over another body, I noticed it was small, too small. I clenched my eyes shut for a moment, saying a quick prayer for the repose of the tiny soul.

As I rounded the corner of the superstore, I saw a crowd of police. Following the trail of smoke, I looked through the legs of the officers; I could see a body lying on the ground, covered in blood. A medical examiner knelt on the side of the body. I was impressed with the speed of the Chicago first responders and deeply saddened this type of mass shooting incident had become commonplace. Most of the people investigating and those helping the wounded were out of sight, working on the front side of the superstore. The body of the man that had been possessed lay awkwardly against a trash dumpster.

A large, black plume of smoke rose from the body and hovered about five feet above the officers, looking like a mushroom. It moved and twisted like a sack full of snakes. One thick ribbon of smoke poured out of the stack, arching over the officers, and landed a few feet in front of me. I watched as the smoke poured out and began to take form. Knowing the rules, I knew it couldn't stay in human form for long. To even be able to manifest as a human meant it was a higher-level demon and not the average chaos demon.

I pulled the rosary from my cross-body bag and squeezed it until I felt the crucifix pierce my skin. Praying the Our Father and a Hail Mary, I watched the demon form into a man. He was dressed in jeans and a black t-shirt. Beautiful in anyone's standard, but all I saw was pure evil. My pulse quickened, as the prayers in my head sped up.

"Lavive," it hissed as we locked eyes.

"Did you miss me?" I asked with a slight smirk, cocking my head to one side and raising an eyebrow.

It grinned, showing off its perfect smile. Sometimes the evilest came in pretty packages. But there was one thing it couldn't fake, and that was the eyes. No matter how hard a demon wanted to take human form, they could never get the eyes right. The eyes were the windows to the soul, which wasn't just an expression. When you're soulless, your windows were black.

"Do you think you can do anything with all these people here? You love these vermin," he said, spitting on the ground. "They, like you, are nothing to us but an entertaining nuisance. We are pumas playing with mice. Do you think the mouse will ever win?" He circled me slowly.

I stiffened, and my palms itched in anticipation of releasing my power. I felt the heat of the Hell fire radiate off its form, and the essence of sulfur burnt my eyes.

"They are stronger than you give them credit; I have witnessed their resilience," I said through gritted teeth.

"Oh, Lavive, when will you learn? Even after all these years, you are still trying to save these things, these humans."

"Don't forget, I am a human; I am these 'things' as you call them. With that in mind, remember that God made us in *His* image; it was *His* love for us that made you jealous in the first place. So really, think about it. We humans have the real power of love; you are only a cast out."

I circled him, and he couldn't contain the aggravation. It settled angrily upon his face. I secretly loved getting them riled up; it made it easier to cast their asses back to Hell.

"That was the past," he growled. "We have learned over the many years that we are stronger than you could ever imagine!"

I smiled wide. "Really?" My voice contained a burst of childlike laughter. It wasn't on purpose, but the thought of a demon being more powerful than God was hysterical.

Falling to the ground, I knelt and prayed the

Our Father before starting the Rite. The demon moaned and stumbled backward, as if an unseen force punched him in the gut. I pressed my hands together as I sang the prayers in the gift of tongues. It sounded like noise in a beautiful melody, but it's said to be the most perfect prayer. My voice sang in words not of this world, tones of highs and lows, all coming together in angelic song. It's as if there was a translation box, somewhere between my brain and mouth, that made my thoughts come out as the most beautiful singsong of prayer I had ever heard.

As I sang, the demon fought to stay standing. Each note attacked a part of its form. I could see his arms thinning and returning to smoke. I knew if he turned back to smoke, he'd be able to travel faster than I could. I had to cast him soon. I continued to pray and rubbed my palms together, allowing the power of prayer to manifest as wisps of light emanating from my palms. I glanced over to the group of officers; none were paying any attention to me. My guardian angel appeared between us and the group of officers. He spread his wings out, making a semi-barrier. It was one of the ways he could help me and still not get in the way of free will—it was a thin line we walked each day.

"Bow to the Lord God, and may He take pity on you," I sang.

"Never!" roared the demon.

I looked over to the officers, and they didn't turn. They must not have been able to hear him. Most people couldn't see demons. I was just a lucky one.

I jumped up from my prayer stance and grabbed his face; my hands were glowing white. "Then return to the Hellfire which you came from, never to enter this world again." I looked into its deep pools of darkness and said with every fiber in my being, "All glory to God in the highest and peace to His people on Earth." Raising one hand toward the Heavens and one still lying on the demon's contorted face, I prayed, "We command you, unclean spirit, whoever you are, along with all your minions, by the mysteries of the incarnation, passion, resurrection, and ascension of our Lord Jesus Christ, by the descent of the Holy Spirit, by the coming of our Lord for judgment, that you tell me by some sign your name and the day and hour of your departure."

The wind whipped around the two of us; I bowed my head in reverence to the Holy Spirit whom I felt near. "By His holy name, we demand your name, unclean spirit!"

"Ipos," it shrieked, twisting its form and transforming into a beast with the head of a lion and the body of an angel. Its feet were webbed and gooselike, standing at least twelve feet, towering over me in stature. I did not falter. I stood steadfast;

my hand outstretched and prayer still on my lips. The light emitted from my palms as I fell to my knees. The power of prayer flowed through me and out of my palms, flowing toward Ipos and wrapping his form in ropes of light.

"Ipos, father of lies and leader of the unclean, depart from here and never return. In the name of the Father and the Son and the Holy Spirit, Amen!" A loud growl echoed throughout my body as the demon collapsed in on itself, bending and contorting smaller and smaller—last to disappear were the black eyes. Then nothing.

Falling to the ground, the air lightened around me. I wiped the sweat from my brow and upper lip with the back of my hand. Suddenly, the entire area was filled with the lovely smell of a million roses; I knew the Holy Mother was near. A sense of calm and relaxation flowed over me as I stood and orientated back to the world around me. The lights and noise seemed distant and softer somehow.

I looked around, and no one had noticed the good and evil showdown that had just occurred, which was a good thing for me anyway. One officer glanced at me; I held my breath and nodded. He nodded back as I looked away. I stood; my legs shook, and my shirt clung to my body. I was spent; it wasn't easy fighting demons. Looking up, I saw my angel floating just above me. His face ever stoic, but I felt his love and healing. I threw him a cocky wink, although he never reacted to my shenanigans; I still liked to mess with him. He didn't have an easy assignment; I could be a holy terror at times.

"Thank you," I mouthed to my angel.

"Excuse me, miss." A loud, male voice thundered in my ears, slamming the world back in focus.

I turned to the voice as my hands instinctively covered my ears. A tall police officer was heading my way, not just any officer either. My eyes widened, as I noticed the large white letters "FBI" across his bulletproof vest.

"Crap!" I turned on my heels and hurried toward the edge of the caution tape. I knew dressed as a fake cop and talking to demons and angels would not go over well with the FBI. I had been successful in avoiding them for the past five years, and I wanted to keep that streak up. As I reached the yellow line of freedom, I felt a hand grab my shoulder. I turned quickly and was face-to-face with the FBI agent; his hazelnut eyes glared at me.

"Can I help you?" I asked and wiggled out of his grasp. *Crap!*

"What are you doing?" he asked and eyed my uniform. *Double crap!*

"Same thing we're all doing, working this case. Now I need to run back to the station for shift change. If you're done interrogating me, I will be on my way." I turned and bent under the caution tape. At five foot two, I was pretty fast, and he couldn't stop me.

"You are free to go," he said to my back. "But first—"

I stopped, and he said, "What's your name?"

"Willot." My brain reeled! I had given him my real last name. "Lavive Willot."

"La-what?"

"La-veeeeve," I said, stretching out the e-sound, but I never stopped walking. I didn't need to look back to know he was watching my every step.

Passing more cars and people, I ducked out of sight at the first building I could find. My heartbeat like a drum in my chest. I didn't get flustered about casting out demons, but going to jail was a whole other level of fear. Why did I give him my real name?

TWO

I unbuttoned the police uniform shirt as I walked, revealing a black tank top. Once undone, I tucked it into my bag. The chill of the Chicago night was welcoming against my skin. Agitated at the FBI agent and his smug face, I rubbed my temples. I'd been questioned by the FBI before, each time talking my way out of the tangled web somehow. But for some stupid reason, I was behaving like this was my first time demon hunting.

"Dammit!" I yelled into the night and hurried my pace. I had no idea why I gave that FBI agent my real name. Why in the Holy Grail would I ever do that? What a stupid thing to do! I knew better; I never gave my real name. It was a rookie mistake and possibly my worst mistake to date.

Rounding another corner, the cheap motel I'd

been staying in for the past three months came into view. When tracking chaos demons, I needed to be in the middle of the hot spot. If that meant sleeping in a flea-infested motel, I did it. I did a lot of things for the hunt.

Pulling out my key, I opened the door and slammed it shut, rattling the thin walls. I gathered my jeans, shirts, leather jacket, holy water, blessed salt, holy oils, and multiple books. Throwing them all into a backpack, I was ready within minutes. It was easy being a minimalist, just the books were heavy. But I couldn't go anywhere without my Bible and the first version of the Rite of Exorcism.

A knock at the door sent me into panic mode. I froze in the middle of the small room, my bag on my back, weighing the options of running. There weren't any back windows to climb out of like in the movies; the door was the only way out.

"Dammit," I whispered while lowering my bag to the ground. I didn't have anywhere to go. As I walked slowly to the door, I created multiple lies about why I was at the shooting and why I was dressed like a police officer.

"I was a person trained in first aid, and I was just trying to help."

"I was a news journalist, trying to get a good look."

Maybe, I was a concerned family member, or maybe he'd believe I was a stripper on my way to a gig? A snort-laugh escaped — even I couldn't believe that one.

I took a deep breath and unhooked the chain lock. As I opened the door, a woman peeked in.

"Hello!" she sang.

I opened the door fully. She was a thin woman, her hair ratted, and red, scabby sores speckled her face and neck. Her tank top was haphazardly tucked in an old pair of jeans; I could see the needle marks on her arms. Definitely not a cop!

"Hey." She nodded and blew a puff of cigarette smoke to the side. "Is John here?"

"No, there's no John here, sorry."

She blinked a few times as if I was going to change my mind.

"Shit! This is the room they gave me on the phone. Damn college kids screwing with me again." She fumbled around in a tattered purse and pulled out a flip phone. "Damn phone is dead! This night is really shitty!" She puffed on her cigarette again and held it in her teeth while she messed with the old phone.

I could tell she hadn't seen a shower in a few days by the looks and smell of her. Well-established dark circles hung under her eyes, as if she hadn't slept in days. Then, there was something else when she looked at me; the blackness of her pupils were swirling. Everything in my being said to shut the damn door, but somehow my mouth didn't get the message.

"What's your name?" I asked and opened the door wide.

"What do you want it to be?" She arched an eyebrow and put a hand on her hip.

"Um, no thanks. I'm not asking for that reason. But I do enjoy the *Pretty Woman* reference."

We both laughed as she lit another cigarette.

"It's Beth; my real name is Beth."

"Hi, Beth, nice to meet you. I'm Lavive, rhymes with believe. I know it's a weird name." I stuck my hand out, and she eyed it as if she'd never shaken someone's hand before. She took it slowly; her grip was like a wilted flower. "Do you want to come in?"

"Why? You said you don't want to party."

"I thought you may want to take a break. It's up to you." I turned and left the door open. I knew a wounded animal needed to be coaxed into moving, and she sure was wounded.

Beth's eyes narrowed, as she took a step inside.

"What's your game? You gonna rob me or something?" I saw the thin, black line of smoke encircle her eye, a tell-tale sign of the damned. As she walked past me, I noticed the odor, sulfur—the smell of Hell.

"No!" I was weighing my options. "I thought maybe you could keep this room; it's paid for, and I gotta run. Stay here, take a hot shower, and watch

TV; rest. Here are some clothes." I pulled out a pair of clean shorts and a t-shirt. "Nothing fancy, but they're clean." I handed her the clothes, which I had carefully sprinkled with Holy Water before pulling them out of my bag.

"Why?" Beth asked again. "What are you getting?" She didn't take the clothes, so I tossed them on the bed next to her. Instinctively, she moved away. Another sign. Aversion to blessed objects.

"Nothing, I get nothing. I want nothing, and sometimes people are just good," I said and sat down next to her on the bed. "We get to choose good over bad, and sometimes, that is a daily choice. What will you choose today?"

Beth looked at me, her eyes wide. "I don't know," she said with tears in her eyes. "I don't know where you been livin', but you ain't finding no good people around Southside."

"Can I pray with you?" I asked as I extended a hand toward her head. She pulled away, but I was faster. I placed my hand on her forehead and traced the sign of the cross. Her back arched, and she let out a low growl. I proceeded to pray over Beth, as the demon that was trying to attach to her fought me. It wasn't a tough case; a minor demon, I supposed, by the way she presented and the way the demon felt. My hands ignited in white light; wisps of light floated from my palms and into Beth.

The power of the Holy Spirit rushed through me. I closed my eyes and prayed in the tongue of angels.

A thin line of black smoke formed from her open mouth and slowly crept its way out of her. I continued to pray as the minor demon was banished back to Hell. Beth collapsed on the bed, her head falling to the side. I felt the power leave, and my hands stopped glowing. I exhaled and wiped my forehead. For some reason, I was supposed to be here at this very minute for her, to save Beth from a lifetime of possession.

She stirred. "What's going on?" she asked and sat up, scooting away from me. By the look she gave me, she didn't remember the past fifteen minutes, which was normal for a demon banishment.

"Here, read this." I tossed a small, white book on the bed and watched as she read the title.

"*God's Not Mad at You*?" She flipped the book back toward me. "You gonna try to get me in some God cult or somethin'? You be nice to me, and I owe you. Is that right?"

"No," I exhaled loudly. "Just look at it. I gotta go. Nice to meet you, Beth." I didn't wait for her to respond. I set the keys on the TV and left her in the room.

The night air had a chill to it. I pulled my jacket out of my bag. I leaned against a fence; my head hung, and a thin layer of sweat covered my skin.

Taking a deep breath, I gathered what strength I had left and pushed forward. I caught the next bus to the main depot, so I could get out of Chicago and away from the FBI.

I'd learned to move around town without a trace—no credit cards, only cash, and only public transportation. It's how I had gone this long without being questioned too much. Although, giving that FBI agent my full name was just about the dumbest thing I had ever done. I prayed the agent wouldn't think I was important enough to look for, but there was something about him that made me think he wouldn't give up so easily.

The Harrison Street Station was bustling, no matter what the time. People and buses moved like choreographed dolls.

"Ticket west."

"Where to?" the ticket agent asked through the glass.

"Don't care, anywhere this can get me and fast." I handed him $150 in cash.

"OK, have fun in Phoenix." He slid the ticket through the slot. "Leaves in ten minutes, better hurry."

I took the ticket and looked around, glancing at the older man behind the glass. His large smile gave me hope for the moment.

I walked fast to the bus lane of the A track that would take me to Phoenix; at least it would be warmer there. That's how I usually traveled, wherever the tide led me, and it was changing. I felt like I was on a very small, rickety boat, but I held on and kept the faith. Since leaving St. Michael's Institute of Exorcism and Spiritual Warfare in New Orleans, I had been roaming the seedy streets of every major city from New York to San Francisco and back. I didn't mind the solitude; I always had my angel with me, even if he didn't talk, and just being there was some solace. Plus, I checked in with Father Pete every now and then for a good confession. Casting demons to Hell wasn't my first choice at a job; but when the Catholic Church asked, I couldn't say no. They had been paying for my travels. I stopped at the diocese in each city, and somehow, they had an envelope of cash waiting for me. I knew I wasn't the only demon hunter on the bankroll, but I was the best. I kept my job to myself; it was safer for everyone.

The world had become a smorgasbord for the demonic, and it was getting harder and harder for each person to choose good over evil.

The overhead speaker called my bus, and I quickened my pace. I looked back toward the ticket counter, and my breath caught in my throat. That FBI agent was talking to the old man who had sold me my ticket.

"Shit!" I pulled my red leather jacket collar up, hiding some of my face. Arriving at the bus, I tried my best to be patient, as the line inched forward. If he didn't see what bus I got on, I would be golden. It was a busy station, and I hoped the ticket counter old guy had a short memory. I relaxed a little with each step toward the bus doors.

"Excuse me, miss." A man's voice called from behind me.

I kept walking forward, playing as if I didn't hear. I handed my ticket to the driver at the bottom of the stairs — so close.

"Hey!" he yelled again, and I looked back. A young man was waving me down with a small, white card in his hand. He trotted up. "You dropped this," he said and pushed the card in my hand.

I thanked him and ducked into the bus. My heart pounded as I looked for an open seat on the already full bus. I found one in the back. It was the only seat — and a window seat at that. I wouldn't normally pick a window seat, especially hiding from the agent, but I had no choice. I nestled in the seat and stared out the dirty glass. I could finally breathe again.

I looked at the white card the guy had handed me. It was my St. Michael prayer card; it must have fallen out of my pocket in the hurry to the bus. I said the prayer on the back and tucked it in my pocket. The bus doors creaked shut as the driver made announcements over the bus speakers. I sank further into the seat. When the bus began to pull away, a smile landed on my face.

Then I saw him. The agent was standing on the platform, looking very intently at my bus that was already pulling away. I slouched down in the seat and watched him, full knowing he didn't have enough on me to stop the bus or arrest me. I let out an audible sigh, as the bus left the depot. My angel floated outside the window; we locked eyes, and a wave of peace fell over me. He was pure beauty; and unlike the demon, his eyes were a pristine blue. When looking into them, it was as if you were seeing a piece of Heaven. I said a guardian angel prayer and thanked him for keeping me safe, as he always did.

THREE

When the bus was a few hours outside Chicago, I finally relaxed. I was grateful to be on the road and away from the demon's aftermath. I was fighting the cause, a cause that has been fought for hundreds of years. A twinge of guilt snuck in; and I wondered if I had been faster or smarter, then I could have stopped the chaos demon before the shooting, before the damned man was killed by the police. So much violence—so much death.

Blinking away the tears, I pulled out my laptop, the only electronic I owned. The bus had public Wi-Fi, and I logged on, searching the news feeds. My heart skipped a beat when I fell upon the story: twenty-eight people! Twenty-eight people had died at the superstore, and many more were injured or in critical condition. I closed my eyes and prayed for the repose of their souls. A vision of the little child I had jumped over flashed in my mind, and I quickly pushed it out.

I looked to my right and saw my angel; he was ever-present, especially in time of sorrow or stress. He floated outside the window of the bus, not affected by the moving vehicle. Angels were in a different space and time than us humans. They could bi-locate and knew everything. I wished he could talk to me, but that wasn't the case. He was always a silent figure in my life, one I was very grateful for. I think over the years he'd gotten used to my ways.

I pulled out my favorite prayer card from the front pocket of my bag.

Angel of God,
My guardian dear.
To Whom His love
Commits me here.
Ever this day,
Be at my side
To light and guard,
To rule and guide.
Amen.

Making the sign of the cross, my mind was clear, and my heart filled with the spirit. From a young age, I could quickly connect with the Trinity, faster and easier than most. I had been gifted with a strong line direct to the Heavens.

Reflecting upon the people that lost their earthly lives at the superstore, I knew they would be welcomed in the next life, and that brought some relief, as much as it could.

I thought of the shooter, the possessed, and prayed for him. Not everyone would or could understand how I prayed for the person who pulled the trigger and hurt so many. But this person hadn't been born bad. He was a victim, too, a victim of the darkness. I knew I couldn't stop him from being possessed, but I would have tried my best. He had free will and chose the evil, but he was just a pawn in the Devil's game of human chess.

It was difficult and sometimes impossible for people to get to a place of true forgiveness; but for me, I could see that the demons were to blame for the wreckage. As I sat alone on the bus, I let the tears fall. I cried for all those who felt the pain and confusion of this shooting and for the entire country. It had become too commonplace, too frequent.

I meditated on this for hours as the bus took me across the Midwest. Sleep eluded me, and the sun began to rise against the Tennessee skyline. We stopped outside Memphis for food and gas. A local diner was attached to the gas station. I wouldn't expect much from the looks of a gas station diner, but I had learned that looks could be deceiving, some of the ugliest things were the best. Plus, it was hard to mess up eggs and grits.

My stomach growled as I stepped off the bus. The dust was thick on the rocky ground of the diner's parking lot. I watched the other passengers walk stiffly to the diner, each of us grunting and stretching. Ten hours on the bus had taken a toll on all of us it seemed.

I sat at the breakfast bar; I really didn't feel like talking to another person, and this was one way to ensure I ate in silence. Visions of the shooting victims and demon deliverance ran through my head as I sipped my coffee.

"Hey there," a man said as he took the seat next to me. I rolled my eyes, not wanting to talk to anyone, but I looked over to be polite.

"Shit," I said as my heart caught in my throat.

"Well, that's one way to say hello," the FBI agent from Chicago said.

I blinked at him, hoping I was imagining this. He sat and ordered a coffee. My mouth hung open as I watched him take a drink of black coffee. He wasn't dressed in his uniform, but a pair of jeans and a white button-down shirt that was haphazardly tucked in. I tried my best to shake off the shock of seeing the FBI agent that had questioned me in Chicago sitting next to me in Tennessee.

"Well, hello," I said and took another sip of coffee.

"How was your drive?" I asked.

"I flew, so it was quite short. I have been waiting for a while."

"For what?"

"Well, you, of course." He eyed me intensely.

"Me?" I faked shock and pretended to clutch imaginary pearls. "Why ever would you want little ole me?" I said in my best Southern accent. He smirked, showing off two very cute dimples. I thought I had just seen a little kink in his FBI armor.

"Why were you in Chicago? Better yet, why were you at the superstore shooting and wearing a fake police uniform? You know it's a federal offense to impersonate an officer of the law."

Dammit, my brain raced, as I tried to recall all the lies I'd come up with—stripper was all I could remember!

"I didn't do anything, and I wasn't hurting anyone. It really doesn't matter why I was there."

"So, you get to decide what matters in an FBI investigation?" He said sternly and straightened his posture. I'd hit a nerve. "What is your full name?" he demanded and pulled out a small notepad from his back pocket.

Dammit again! I was accomplishing one thing, and that was pissing off the agent. Might as well really get him revved up. I decided to take a little satisfaction in annoying him. "Lavive. My name is Lavive. I told you that already back in Chicago, and I wasn't lying."

"Really?" he asked.

I shook my head yes.

"Then why can't I find anything on you in the system? No license? No home address?"

"I don't drive, and I live on the streets." I smirked.

"No credit cards?" he pressed

"Cash only."

"No cell phone? Come on!" He raised his hands.

"Nope, no cell phone either." I put my elbows on the counter and cradled my face in my palms. "Anymore super intrusive questions?" I asked and couldn't help but smile.

"What are you running from?" he asked

"I'm not running from anyone! If anything, I run to those that need me."

"Who needs you, Lavive?" he asked with a snide tone. "Who needs a white-haired, blue-eyed fake cop?"

I clenched my teeth as I felt my blood pressure raise. I knew he was just trying to get me upset. Upset people lashed out and told more than expected. It was a typical tactic, and damn, it was working.

"We've been tracking you for a while." He passed a manila folder to me. I picked it up and thumbed through it. There were clippings of the fire in Chicago, a few other events in New York, and some of a bombing at a mosque in Jersey. Notes were scribbled about a white-haired woman at each.

"Seems like you have me mistaken with another woman with white hair. I don't know anything about these events." I lied. "What is your name, Agent?"

"Special Agent O'Connely," he said and passed me a card. I read the card.

"Tanner?" I asked.

"Yes, Tanner O'Connely," he said calmly. He was good about only giving me exactly what I asked for. I had been able to advert cops before, but this agent was different; and it wasn't just the dimples. To follow me from Chicago to Tennessee, he had to have some agenda. I looked at him, noticing his deep-set eyes and dark brows. He was a handsome man, for a special agent.

"I like Tanner. It softens the hard-ass FBI agent persona a little." I tried my most flirty smile on him.

"I assure you, Lavive, there is nothing soft about me."

I felt my cheeks flush. For the first time, he fully

smiled. His smile lit his dark eyes; his teeth were perfectly straight and those dimples! A girl could get lost in that smile, but I wasn't your typical girl.

I broke my gaze on his adorable dimples and looked around the diner. The others were loading up onto the bus, and I hadn't even eaten! I asked for a bagel and any other pastry they had to go and paid the waitress.

"Well, Special Agent Tanner O'Connely, I would love to stay and chat, but I have a bus to catch. You can stalk me later." Laughing, I slid off the stool and hurried to the door, pastries in hand.

"I still have questions. You are an observer of the shooting. I need a statement" he said, standing.

"Men are never satisfied," I said and winked. "Listen, I didn't get to the scene until after your colleagues had already taken down the shooter. I was there just to help, that's all. Nothing else. Now, if you'll excuse me, till next time, Tanner." I waved and walked out the door, hustling to the bus. I was the last one to take my seat in the back. Looking out the window, I saw Tanner, standing, arms crossed and very broody. He certainly was cute when he was pissed.

The bus pulled away, and I settled into the seat. I took a bite of the bagel as my mind swam with questions. How did he have a file on me? What else did they know? I was feeling exposed and knew that agent O'Connely wasn't going to let this go.

But, if he knew the truth, he'd lock me up in the nearest insane asylum. Being a demon hunter for the Catholic Church isn't a "normal" job you just told people about over a casual dinner. Since my eighth-grade confirmation, I had been able to see angels and demons, and no one had ever believed me. That was until Father Pete in New Orleans.

He was understanding and open to my unique situation. It was a great gift and with it, came solitude. Only a few could ever understand what I did for them and for the world.

I laid my head back against the seat, my angel hovered above me. I smiled. Looking into his eyes, the world seemed better, lighter, where FBI special agents didn't bother me. In his eyes, there was just a lovely calmness, and I let myself get lost in it.

FOUR

A day later the bus made its final stop in Phoenix, Arizona. I ached all over; forty hours on a bus was not my version of a good time. I needed a shower and a real bed — badly. The bus stopped at the depot; it wasn't a big as Chicago and certainly not as busy. Grabbing my bag, I shuffled my way off the bus, following all the other passengers. It was late afternoon as the sun hung low in the desert sky.

There was a small motel across the street; but by the looks of it, it was one of those pay-by-the-hour motels. As the other passengers got into cars and met family, I walked alone to the motel. I got a room for a few days with the last bit of cash I had on me. I'd stop by the Diocese of Phoenix and pick up more cash soon.

I showered off the stink of demon, sweat and public bus. Living out of one suitcase didn't leave me much room for anything but necessities, although I did splurge on one thing. Years ago, when in Dauphin Island, Alabama, I went to a little surf shop and found a perfume called Inis, the scent of the sea. I fell in love and bought the shower gel and oils. Breathing in the scent reminded me of the little island and the ocean, which I loved so much.

The water from the shower ran over my face, and I imagined being at the beach with the sun, sand, and waves of the ocean. I always thought of the waves of the ocean like the heartbeat of the earth—a never-ending, constant force. Even the sound of the pounding waves is reminiscent of the heartbeat heard in our mother's womb. The perfectness of the ocean always calmed my spirit.

Wrapping in a scratchy, cheap towel, I made it to the bed and collapsed. The past two days caught up to me quickly, and without any effort at all, I passed out.

*　　　*　　　*

An obnoxiously loud knock at the door was a terrible way to wake up. Stumbling out of bed, still half asleep, I wobbled my way to the door. "What the hell!" I said, cracking the door open, one eye still squinted shut. A badge was thrust in my face, and I let out a sigh.

"What do you want? I am sleeping!"

"You really aren't afraid of anything are you?" Tanner asked and lowered his badge.

"If you're trying to scare me with a badge in my face, try again, Agent." I leaned my face against the door jam. "What do you want, Tanner? Obviously, you really need me, or are you just following buses around the US?"

"Can I come in?"

I looked down and realized I had lost my towel on the way to the door and was buck naked! That perked me right out of my sleepy daze.

"Just a sec," I said through the crack and closed the door. I got dressed quickly, pulled my unruly dreadlocks up into a high bun, and wiped my eyes on the scratchy towel.

I opened the door and noticed the cool air and rising sun. I had slept the entire evening and night away, I must have been tired. Tanner stood, dressed in a black suit and white button-down shirt, a few buttons opened at the top. His put-together look was a stark comparison to my look of thrown-together mess of a traveling hobo that I had going on.

"Ok, now tell me, what are you doing here?"

"Looking for you obviously."

"Are you seriously stalking me?" I put my hands on my hips and tilted my head to the side.

"I wouldn't call it stalking. Just monitoring."

"Well, Agent, you don't need to monitor anything! Bye." I slammed the door, but it didn't slam. Tanner's foot was in the way. *Persistent little ass*, I thought.

"I just want to ask you some questions; then I will leave, promise," Tanner said, his chestnut eyes drawn into a most serious expression.

"Fine," I said sharply. "We can talk—out on that picnic table—there." I pointed to a table about ten feet away. I ducked out of my room and locked the door behind me.

"Thanks, Lavive," he said as we walked. He took a handkerchief out of his pants pocket and blotted his forehead.

"Do you always carry around a hankie?" I eyed the white cloth. "Seems a bit old school for these days."

Tanner wrung the handkerchief in his hands. "Yeah, I do. My grandfather taught me to always carry one. He said that they are the only fabric that will encounter great joy, true sadness, and immense pain. Always to be pocketed for another day."

He placed the handkerchief in his pocket, and I felt an odd pang in my gut. *What the hell was that?* I wanted to know more about this handsome agent who had stalked me across the USA. There was something about him that drew me in like a riptide.

I shook my head, pushing out the thoughts. What I really needed to do was get this hot agent out of my life as soon as possible. The last thing I needed was a distraction when demon ass-kicking.

"So, Agent Tanner, what can I do for you?" I asked for the hundredth time and took a seat on top of the picnic table.

"We never got to finish our conversation at the restaurant outside Memphis. You still owe me a real explanation as to why you were at the shooting in Chicago. Not to mention all the other devastating events where you have been the past few years."

"I did tell you the real story," I lied.

"I can tell when you lie; you twirl your hair." He motioned to my fingers wrapped around an unruly dread that had escaped the high bun. I tucked the hair back up and ignored his observation.

"You wouldn't believe me, Agent."

"Please call me Tanner."

"Well, Tanner, you would not believe me if you knew the whole story."

"Try me, Lavive, what I have seen might surprise you. At this point in my life, I believe anything is possible." He sat on the table next to me. I noticed the St. Michael the Archangel medal around his neck. Maybe he would believe me?

"So…" He motioned for me to start the story.

Every nerve in my body screamed to stop; but I glanced over to my angel, and he nodded. It took me a minute for my brain to process it—my angel actually sort of talked to me! He never does that! A nod from him was like a loud scream from God Himself. In the shock of it all, I started blurting out the truth to Tanner—the actual truth.

"I wasn't there by accident."

"I assumed as much," Tanner interrupted.

I gave him a dirty look, and he was quick to respond with, "Sorry, go on."

"I suppose I start at the beginning." I sat cross-legged. Still apprehensive, I looked toward my angel again, and he nodded again! My apprehension disappeared. "My parents, what I know of them. Well, my mother was half Japanese and half Caucasian. She'd been a nun at one time but discerned out for my father. My dad was African with an albino recessive gene, hence the white hair." I motioned to the twisted bun of hair on top of my head.

"The two of them met on the grounds of the convent and fell in love. A scandal in the church, as you can imagine! They were released from their duties. My mother, Mi Sun Sing or Sunny for short became pregnant soon after and before the wedding!" I wiggled my eyebrows. "Which only enhanced the drama around her in the church.

Mistakes were made, and life got hard. After my father died in a car accident, my mom tried her best; but I suppose she wanted me to have a better life. Eventually, she decided adoption was for my best interest. I heard that, years later, she was able to go back into the convent in some capacity; I don't know for sure." I rubbed my hands together. "I don't know where she is or if she is even alive." I heard my voice soften and wiped my eyes with the back of my hand.

Tanner produced the handkerchief in record time. "Always prepared," I said and laughed a bit while taking the hanky, blotting my eyes.

"Thank you for telling me about your parents," Tanner said, taking back his handkerchief.

"Yeah, well, you should feel pretty damn special. Only a handful of people on this Earth know my story." I nudged him with my elbow.

"Oh, I do!" He nudged me back. "But, why were you at the superstore in Chicago?"

"Getting there." I held my hand up. "Growing up in foster care, I was alone for most of my life. It didn't help that I was, well, different."

"Kids can be mean," Tanner interjected.

"It wasn't all just about looks. I could handle the teasing about my hair, but it was the other stuff that was really hard."

"What stuff?" Tanner probed.

"I will tell you, but you have to hear all of it

before you judge me." I gave him an annoying gaze.

He held up his hands. "Ok, I'll try to shut it!" His smile was warm, and I leaned a few inches closer.

"Like I said, I was different—not just the slant in my blue eyes or the white of my hair against my dark skin. It was the other gifts the Spirit bestowed upon me that gave me the most trouble."

By the look on Tanner's face, I could tell he was very confused.

"When I was in eighth grade, I had my confirmation. I was living with a nice family at that time. They had a little party for me; it was great." Remembering that family and their love brought back great memories; my life was so different before that day, almost normal.

"The little party was in the backyard, where everyone was having a great time, which was the first time I saw one—"

"Saw what?" Tanner asked as his hand wrapped around mine. I stiffened when he touched me. He squeezed my hand, and I let him hold it as I continued.

"I didn't know what it was at first. It was attached to one of the adults at the party; he seemed to not see it. No one saw it, but I could see it. A black mass hovered around the man, like if snakes were made of smoke and wriggled around in the air. I was terrified, but I couldn't stop watching the darkness twist and turn around the man. It moved as the man moved; it followed his every step." I took a deep breath and squeezed Tanner's hand. "That was the first demon I'd ever seen, but not nearly the last." I looked at Tanner's face, and he watched me with intense eyes.

"I was terrified with what I saw and felt about that man. I heard years later that he killed his wife and two sons before turning the gun on himself. I wondered if the mass of smoky snakes had anything to do with his terrible actions. Later in life with more experience, I learned that yes, it did; and no, I couldn't have done anything at that moment. It was an integrated demon, and I was only fourteen."

"I know what integration means."

"You do? Most lay persons don't know anything about the possession process. It's not like it's covered with core math or anything." I looked at him and smiled. It had been so long since anyone understood me.

"Yes, the integrated demon is accepted or welcomed, and the two had become one," Tanner explained, and I nodded. "I was trained in deliverance prayer and healing prayer with the Archdiocese of Chicago. It's all very confusing and terrifying, but I do have some understanding."

"Why were you in training?" I asked.

"I once was on a different path, as a young man I had grand ideas of being in religious life."

"Like a priest?" I let go of his hand.

He laughed. "It was a long time ago; things happened, and my path took a very different direction."

"I can see that, Agent O'Connely. Do you still attend Mass regularly?" I knew it was an intrusive question, but one that would tell me if he still practiced.

"No." Tanner looked to the ground as his voice thinned.

I didn't press any further. "Well, this will be much easier than I thought!" I smiled wide. "After the first sight of the demon, I would see them and angels periodically. It wasn't all the time, and I had no control when, where, or how." I glanced to my right as my angel floated nearby. I didn't think Tanner needed to know that bit of information. "Most people can't see what I see. The Spirit gifted me with many charisms, like being able to see angels and demons and speaking in tongues. At about eighteen, I decided to embrace my gifts and stop fighting and ignoring them. I met a great priest that taught me about the strange world only I could see and how to battle for good and fight evil. We trained, and I learned how to hone my tracking abilities, how to pray, and the Rite of Exorcism." I didn't tell him about my glowing hands and the light power I could harness. Some things were better kept a secret.

"How do you stay so calm with all of this? Aren't you afraid?"

"Sometimes, but it's usually for the people I love, not for myself. I have faith. I see the truths and with that, comes great relief. I don't need to fear the unknown because it's known to me."

"So, you were at the shooting chasing a demon?" Tanner's forehead wrinkled, and he wrung his hands together.

"Sometimes the bad people are not just bad; there are reasons for their actions. I was there chasing down a chaos demon. It was attached to the shooter and had been responsible for a fire on the north side a month earlier. That's why I was there. The fake police uniform, well, I dress the part to get close. I wasn't hurting anyone; on the contrary, I was helping! The police shot the man, but the demon survived. I was able to cast him to Hell before it could attach to another person." I felt myself puff my chest out a bit. It wasn't often I got to share my life with anyone outside the institute.

Tanner sat quietly for a while. I assumed he was processing all the data I had just dumped on him. It was heavy; it was even heavy for me, and I did it for a living. I watched him stare off into the night until he was ready to talk.

"You speak about this with such conviction, I

almost believe it — almost." Tanner's tone had suddenly turned flat; his face was stoic and suddenly hardened.

"What?" I couldn't understand the words coming out of his mouth.

"Lavive, the FBI says and does what it needs to in order to get what we need. I don't believe you were there hurting or helping. I could arrest you for impersonating a police officer, but I'm not. Stay out of places you don't belong. You are no threat; you are just a religious fanatic." He actually looked down his nose at me! "I have wasted my time." He hopped off the picnic table and dusted off his pants.

"Goodbye, Ms. Willot."

FIVE

"What the actual eff just happened?" I watched Tanner walk to his car. I was stunned by the sheer coldness of his demeanor. I glared at my guardian angel, "You nodded, why did you nod if he was completely full of shit? Dammit!"

I jumped off the table and followed Tanner to his car. He was opening the door when I yelled, "Hey!"

He looked up; his face was still emotionless. I stomped toward the car, fully ready to kick his ass if needed.

"You can't treat people like that! You can't just pretend to care to get your way then—boom—drop bombs like some nuke test zone. This isn't North

Korea! I am a person, a human, with feelings and emotions."

"I understand you're upset, Ms. Willot, but this is just protocol," he said and opened his car door, sliding into the black Buick with ease.

I slammed my opened hand on the car hood; my heart raced. "Well, your protocol is SHIT!" I didn't mean to scream like a crazy person, but that's exactly how it came out. My fists were balled, and I was really feeling like I could kick his ass if needed—no matter if he was a foot taller and about 75 pounds heavier. I was fired up!

Tanner closed his door and smirked as he pulled out of the motel parking lot—smirked! I flipped him the bird and stormed back in my room. I slammed the door, opened it again, and slammed it over and over. "UGH!" I stomped around the tiny room fuming. I imagined steam coming out of my ears, like those old cartoons.

"What a liar!" I yelled and continued to pace the room. I looked around for my angel, and he was nowhere to be found. "Of course," I yelled. "Coward!" I screamed into the empty room. "You are all nod this and that; and when the shit hits the fan, you disappear! Nice, real nice."

Finally calming to a level where I could at least sit down, I flopped onto the bed. Recalling the past hour, everything I had told Tanner, all the private feelings and total honesty, I felt so stupid, so used. I couldn't believe I actually trusted him! The kicker was I would have never told that stupid agent anything if my angel wouldn't have nodded—now what? I couldn't even trust an angel? The thought frightened me; but if true, I couldn't trust another person—ever!

I lay on the bed, questioning my every movement over the two days. My angel appeared and hovered above me. I gave him the dirtiest look I could muster and turned to my side. In complete protest, I closed my eyes and stayed there in full-on tantrum mode. I still felt his presence. He warmed the air around me, cocooned in love and light. It was hard to be upset with him, but I tried.

I flipped over to my back; he still hovered above. I crossed my arms and bit my cheek. "Why did you approve of Agent Tanner if he was going to be a total dill-hole?" I asked.

The angel lit up; he was always light, but he really lit up! He raised his hand, and as it neared me, I fought the urge to reach out. I knew I couldn't touch him no matter how badly I wanted to. Looking him in the face, it glowed like translucent twinkly lights; he was beautiful.

The thought came to me: *God has a plan, and sometimes, that plan is a mystery and impossible to understand. Accepting what is can be a very difficult part of being human but essential for my work. Even if I don't like it, I don't understand it, I had to accept*

Tanner and whatever path our relationship or non-relationship took.

I calmed down as fast as I blew up; my angel had that effect on me. I knew in the end, there was a grandmaster plan; and unfortunately, I didn't know how it was going to end. I had been gifted many supernatural powers, but prophetic vision wasn't one of them.

I rolled off the bed, and my stomach growled loudly. I decided to get something to eat and chew on the acceptance issue a bit more. There was a Waffle House across the street, a dive diner with amazing hash browns. Grabbing my cross-body bag that I always had on me, I never knew when I might need my mini kit for demons. Some holy water and a rosary were inside, just in case. I locked up the motel room, walking slowly through the warm desert air. It was late morning, and I was starving.

Walking into the diner, a bell dinged. A few patrons sat in the small diner. I noticed a striking black man in a black turtleneck sitting at a booth by the door.

"Hola!" a ridiculously beautiful young Mexican woman sang from behind the counter. Her raven hair was pulled up to a high ponytail, and red lips accentuated her high cheekbones and perfectly sculpted eyebrows. "Seat yourself, por favor."

I took a seat at one of the booths at the windows

and watched the young Mexican beauty bounce around the diner; her laugh and enthusiasm were infectious. She was a beacon of light in that tiny diner. I wondered what her story was and how she ended up in a Waffle House in Phoenix, but I didn't ask. I needed food and to mull on my own issues with Tanner.

I watched people walk up and down the street outside; most were homeless, and some were "working" girls and others, the bosses. Spending the past five years on the streets, it was easy for me to pick out the different players.

"Hola, señorita, what can I get you?" asked the pretty waitress. She must have been in her early twenties but was dressed in an old-fashioned white diner uniform with a lace-trimmed apron. I could see she'd be popular around here; she could stop a train with those looks. The name tag perfectly placed on her ample chest read, Rosa. Fitting.

"Hi, just a second." I glanced over the menu as Rosa tapped her pen on the tablet of paper she held. "I guess the stack of waffles, two eggs, and coffee. Oh, and can I have a side of cheese hash browns?"

"You want both waffles and hash browns?" she asked and raised her eyebrows.

I nodded and wiggled a little in my seat.

"Little thing like you? Oh, honey, we're going to

have to roll you out of here! Oh, ¡Dios mío!" She let out a deep laugh. "Coffee?" She lifted the pot she'd brought with her to the table.

"Yes, gracias," I said, and Rosa smiled wide; her beautiful white teeth shone bright against her lush, red lips. I felt a little envy in my belly. I would love to have her looks.

"De nada. I'll be right back with it." Rosa bounded away, and I sat back in the seat.

My stomach growled again. I tried to remember the last time I had had a proper meal. Outside of Memphis the first time Tanner the Agent showed up, I'd only had time to grab some pastries. Stalker. I internally rolled my eyes and played with the sugar packets on the table. I was still mad at myself for trusting him. Digging in my cross-body bag, I looked to make sure I had some cash left to pay for my food. I really needed to get to the Diocese of Phoenix. I found a crumpled up twenty-dollar bill at the bottom of my bag.

The ding of the door caught my attention; it swung open and a woman with long, black hair stumbled in. She wore a pair of cutoff shorts and a white tank top with a very visible hot pink bra. She whipped her head around, looking frantically in the diner. I watched her closely. A quick glance at her dilated eyes told me she was high as a kite. But there was something off about the girl—not just that she was high, not just that she rushed into a diner like a tornado. There was something out of place. The clothes she wore were clean, and her shoes and gold clutch were authentic, not a knockoff of Louis Vuitton. I could tell a fake, and those were not fakes. Her hair was clean and perfectly flat ironed. She was thin, most likely from drug use, but she didn't have the typical signs of overuse. I watched her sit at the breakfast bar, still glancing around the diner, looking for something or someone.

She had money, or someone she knew did. Although she stood out to me, the others in the diner didn't even seem to notice her. I watched as she ordered a coffee with shaking hands. She sat on the stool, constantly adjusting her top and shorts and then running her hands through her hair. She rummaged through her purse a few times, pulling out gum.

"Here you go, señorita." Rosa served me the waffles, eggs and hash browns. It all looked fantastic. I dove into the hash browns like I hadn't eaten in weeks. Each bite bigger than the next, it was glorious. If you could love food, this was love. "You enjoy those hash browns." Rosa laughed and walked back toward the kitchen. I hadn't even noticed she was watching me devour my food and didn't care—I was starving!

As I ate, I kept an eye on the girl with the long, black hair at the breakfast bar. She took a gulp of coffee, looked out the window, and checked her phone a few times. It didn't take an FBI agent to know she was waiting for someone, probably her dealer. I hated that drugs were the first thing I thought of, but I was usually right.

Rosa bounced around the diner, taking the black man's order.

I looked to my right, and my angel hovered near. I was relieved to see him. I concentrated on the diner, noticing a light form above the girl. It started off small and grew to encompass the entire area above her. It was her guardian angel. He was just as beautiful as mine, shining a light rose pink color. I watched, completely confused. I had never seen an angel glow pink. Usually, my angel was blue; and all the ones I had seen prior to this girl's angel were also blue, unless the person was close to death. Then the guardian angel turned a maroon color. Pink? Pink wasn't a color I'd seen before. I made a mental note to ask Father Pete about the pink angel.

The pink angel floated down to hover behind the girl; its wings spread and began to wrap her in a cocoon of feathers and pink light. I shot my angel a confused look. This was very abnormal.

Another ding at the door pulled my attention to a man walking into the diner. He wore a tattered t-shirt and dirty jeans. He sat at the breakfast bar, a few stools down from the girl with the pink angel. I watched them exchange eye contact and wondered if he was the person she'd been waiting for, but they never talked to each other. The diner's air was suddenly stale, not just the greasy food. This scent was the unique smell of sulfur. It started off as a hint and grew to encompass the entire diner. My eyes watered, and my throat burned.

I straightened and scanned the dining room for the source of the stench. The prayers started in the back of my mind, and my palms began to burn. There was a demon near! I sat on my hands, afraid they would start glowing.

A faint flicker of smoke, like a ribbon, caught my eye, as it crept under the front door and entered the diner. It moved like a wicked snake across the floor and went to the breakfast bar. The angel's pink wings stiffened around the girl, turning to a dark maroon color, as it tightened its wrap on her. It was trying to protect her, but I knew there was only so much it could do. The girl, like every human, had free will, no matter how stupid.

The black tendrils of smoke weaved their way up the stools and around the girl and the other man at the counter, reaching the two unsuspecting human ankles. I watched tendrils crawl up the girl's legs, twitching and turning around and around. The two customers didn't seem to notice; people rarely paid attention when evil was upon them. Once someone was already drowning in evil, then the thought that something might be wrong came to them. The black ribbon wrapped around her thighs and squeezed. Her angel tightened his bright maroon wings. By the look of it, she was in danger.

Her head snapped up forcefully, and she turned quickly toward the door. She threw down a few dollars and ran out of the diner, the smoke disintegrating as she ran. Her angel lagged behind her. The other man at the bar seemed unaffected and kept drinking his coffee, not even noticing the girl. I jumped up, grabbed my cross-body bag, and ran toward the door. Turning, I yelled to Rosa, "I will be right back — promise!"

I didn't wait for an answer and ran out of the building, searching to the right and left for the girl. Something powerful was calling her. My palms burned with power, as I said a prayer. I rounded the corner of the building and saw the girl a few blocks ahead of me. She was bent over and talking to someone in a black car. I put my hands in my jacket pockets and walked as fast as I could without looking crazy. The sun began to beat down in the midmorning light.

I quickened my pace; my hands still stuffed in my pockets. I felt the power of prayer flow through me. I knew I was close to a demon, the hair on the back of my neck stood on end, and sweat gathered on my brow. Black smoke poured out of the car, fogging the area and engulfing the girl. I couldn't tell who was in the car; the smoke distorted my view of the area. I saw her lean into the car. I pulled my hands out of my pockets; they were glowing white with power. The smoke ran from the light, as I closed in.

I was about five feet away from her — so close I could almost touch her — almost. Suddenly, the car revved its engine; the girl jerked back and looked at me. Her eyes quickly focused on my glowing hands. She seemed to be in a trance of some sort. She bent down, and then she was gone, pulled into the car through the window! Flinging myself at her, I grazed her foot as she disappeared into the car. It sped off, and I fell to the pavement.

SIX

"Dammit!" I yelled as I peeled myself off the concrete, taking a few steps toward the speeding car. My knees and palms ached while I walked. When the car was out of sight, I checked out my injuries. They weren't too bad, just scrapes and a trickle of blood on my knees. I'd live.

I hobbled my way back to where the girl disappeared into the car and bit my lower lip. That was a powerful demon, not a lower-level demon. Lower-level demons couldn't move humans like the girl had disappeared into the car; that was a strong one for sure. I had run into higher-level demons in my past, and Father Pete had taught me about some of the history of demon hierarchy.

Just like angels, demons had their own choirs. The angels traditionally had nine choirs or levels from the seraphim to an angel, such as my guardian angel. Demons, who were the fallen angels, were thought to have their own hierarchy, with Satan being at the lead and at least two levels that I had seen or studied, the higher- and lower-level demons. I learned a little more at each hunt about the demonic world.

My angel was there, floating near the street where the girl was taken. I looked down and saw the girl's gold purse lying on the ground. I picked it up and searched for some identification or anything that could tell me her name. There wasn't an ID in the small purse. I shoved it in my bag. I did find her phone and turned it over and over in my hand. Luckily, it didn't have a lock on the screen; so, I dialed 911 and began to formulate a believable story.

*   *   *

Hours later, I was finally back in my room. My body ached, and my head pounded. The officer who had arrived didn't seem to be interested in what he assumed was a missing junkie. I tried to assure him that it was more of a kidnapping than just a drug deal gone bad; after all, it was early in the day! He took the report and her phone; but I didn't have a name or even a license plate number, so there wasn't much they could do at that moment. I was sure they would trace the phone and find her name eventually.

I held the girl's gold purse. I had kept it once I'd determined there was nothing for the police in it. I was sure they would disagree. I turned it over and held it to my chest.

The day turned into night as the evening hours dragged on. I pondered where the girl could be and if she was safe. Around midnight, I fell asleep.

The clamor of people and barrage of lights pouring through the window pulled me out of sleep. Stumbling out of bed, I went to the window. My heart beat hard in my chest. The parking lot was full of police vehicles, an ambulance, and one fire truck. I sucked in a deep breath. "Shit!"

I quickly gathered my things. Every time I'd seen a bunch of cops, I'd run off to the next safe place; but there was demon activity going on around this motel and diner. I had to stay put.

I studied them again outside my window. The uniformed and street-clothed officers puttered around the parked cars. I relaxed a little. Whatever had happened was over. I knew the difference between an active scene and a recovery.

The ambulance doors were opened, and a gurney was taken out and wheeled around the corner of the motel. I put down my bag, went out, and locked the door to follow the gurney. Rounding the corner, I watched two EMTs lower the gurney to the ground. A faint smell of sulfur lingered in the air. I peered around one of the EMTs and saw the body; the long, dark hair and pink bra were the first things I noticed. The arms and legs were spread out in a haphazardly manner; she looked like a doll thrown to the floor.

It was her — the girl from the diner, the girl who had been ripped off the streets into the black car, the girl with the gold purse. That girl was dead.

My eyes stung; I replayed the day in my mind, trying to find a way it could have ended differently. I noticed the time; it had only been twelve hours since she was taken in that black car. I should have been faster. I should have acted in the diner instead of letting her get outside. I should have done something, anything more to save that girl. I pressed my back against the cold brick building and watched them put her body in a black bag, covering her face. They loaded her onto the gurney, the familiar clicks of metal on metal stretched the gurney to its standing position.

They wheeled and loaded her into the back of the ambulance. I watched as I walked slowly back to my room. There were plenty of other motel gawkers; no one had noticed me following the dead girl.

"Hey!" I jumped, as I ran into a chest. Looking

up, I saw it was the same officer whom I gave the report to yesterday, the same officer who didn't give a damn about the kidnapped girl.

"Ms. Willot, we spoke yesterday. I am Officer Matthews," he addressed me formally. "I wanted to inform you—"

"I see what happened! I told you yesterday she was in trouble, and you did nothing! Now, now, that girl is dead!" I balled my fists.

"I did, miss, I did what I could. I promise I did," he stuttered.

"Right. I'm sure you really combed the streets for her." I rolled my eyes and nudged past Officer Matthews.

"That's no way to treat a fellow officer, Lavive." Tanner leaned against my motel door.

"What the hell are you doing here? I thought you left. I mean I'm only a 'religious fanatic' and don't know anything. Right?" I yelled. "Get off my door!"

Tanner raised his eyebrows and grinned a little, showing off his dimples. I tried not to notice, but I totally noticed. He slid to the side and gracefully motioned for me to enter my own room. I was in no mood for his antics. I rolled my eyes and huffed past him, unlocking my door, and slammed it on both of them.

"Arg!" I threw my key across the room. "Why can't you help me, or her, or tell me anything?

Something!" I yelled at my angel.

Its expression never faltered; its beautiful face focused on mine. Raising its hands, he cupped my face. I started to move back, but he kept a hold of me. He'd never touched me before; he felt like silk and feathers had gotten together and made a baby, and that baby was his hands. But why? Why was he touching me now? I had been through tough times before, and he had never touched me. I made sure he wasn't turning maroon in color.

His eyes focused on mine. They shown as bright as a million stars, filling my vision and the room with light. I watched the colors in them move as if a distant galaxy was forming into existence—a perfect dance of dreams, love, light, and energy. A calming force washed over me, and my body instinctively relaxed.

"Thank you," I whispered with tears in my eyes. This was the first time he'd let me see so much of the Heavens. Maybe I just had to ask? Could it have always been that simple?

I instantly tensed up at the knock on the door; I just knew it was Tanner. I was in no mood for his asshat behavior. No matter if he was eye candy hot, I was still mad. He knocked again. I prayed for acceptance. I knew he'd persist; he did, after all, travel across the US to chase me down the first time. The third knock confirmed it. Groaning loudly, I opened the door.

"What!" I yelled louder than even I expected.

"Well, that isn't a very nice greeting." Tanner straightened his back and raised his brow.

"I don't have time for your shit, Tanner! What do you want?" I rubbed my forehead, feeling a massive headache brewing.

"Well, I am here two-fold. One, to check on you, and the other to see if you knew anything about the girl we found oddly close to your room— dead from an overdose." He pulled out a notepad and pen. "Can I come in?" He asked in the politest tone.

I knew he wasn't leaving; my head was pounding. Feeling defeated, I reluctantly said yes.

I left the door half open and crawled into the bed, burying my face in a pillow. "Close the curtains please; my head is killing me."

"Certainly." Tanner obliged and took a seat in the empty chair.

I took my face out of the pillow and laid on my side. "Last time we talked, you acted so interested and truly concerned for me, then bam! An abrupt turn into asshole land!"

"Lavive, I'm sorry about the way I acted yesterday. I didn't mean to come off so—"

"Ass-hole-ish!"

Tanner grinned. "Yes, so ass-hole-ish. I was just doing my job, but I could have handled myself better. I am sorry."

I pursed my lips and narrowed my eyes. "I bet

you are." I was skeptical; he'd need to prove himself if he ever wanted me to trust him again. "What are you really doing here? The truth!"

Tanner nodded and leaned back into the chair. "I was flying back to DC when I got a call about another death here in Phoenix. Apparently, this is the eleventh overdose in eight days, which is extremely out of the ordinary, even for this neighborhood. I'm here to investigate if this is a serial poisoner."

"You mean someone is deliberately killing these people?" I remembered the coils of black ribbon-like smoke that led the girl to the car that took her. "Who?" I asked, but my gut told me it was a very powerful drug demon. What I didn't know was its vessel. "Why are you looking into this?"

"Well, yes, I think there is one person or one group. We don't know who. I am here because this is my specialty."

"What's that?"

"My specialty?"

"Yes, what is it that you do for the FBI?" I sat up, my head still hurting, but I needed to know everything he knew.

"I am a special agent of domestic terrorism. I investigate any issue that could possibly turn into a mass event, such as the Chicago shooting or this potential poisoning epidemic. I'm hoping you can help me with this one. I know you saw the girl last night."

"What was her name?" I asked in a small voice.

"Emily," Tanner answered and lowered his eyes. He waited a few minutes before asking, "You saw Emily last night, right?"

"Right," I answered, but my mind was elsewhere.

"You reported her being kidnapped. I spoke with the officer you talked to. I know there was more to the story. What actually happened?" Tanner eyed the lump under the covers on the bed next to me. I instinctively put my hand on the gold purse.

"This was hers. She dropped it when they took her," I said, pulling out the purse from the covers.

"Who took her?" he asked and held out his hand for the purse. "And why didn't you give this to Officer Matthews?"

"If I knew that, you wouldn't be here." I handed him the bag. "There is nothing in here for the police, I checked."

"Are you sure you're the best to make that decision?" Tanner raised an eyebrow.

"It's already made; get over it, Tanner!" I rubbed my temples. "I do know it was a demon that took her," I paused to look at his face. "No matter what you think."

He just listened.

"It was a very powerful demon. I think it was a

drug demon, but usually the drug demons I've run into are lower-level demons. This one last night yielded great power, certainly not a lower-level demon."

"Did you see an actual person, a human?" he asked.

"No, if I did, I could have expelled the demon and would have saved Emily. I didn't see anyone but her." I pang of guilt hit me. I should have been faster for her.

"You are a very intriguing woman, a hard ass and a big ole softy. I find that fascinating," he said in a low voice with his head tilted to one side.

"I'm awesome," I replied and let out an uncomfortable laugh. "Are you going to open the purse?"

"Oh, yes." He held the small, gold purse in his large hands and popped open the clasp. He rummaged around. "Well, that's not much to go on," he said, snapping the purse shut.

"Really?" I asked. "Nothing struck you odd about the contents?"

"Not really. A few packs of cinnamon gum and some lip stuff isn't telling me anything."

"Right!" I threw my hands up. "You're not a woman, but women don't carry much when we go out. However, there are some staples, like cash and an ID, plus some face powder."

"Her ID was found on the body."

"Let me guess, tucked into her pink bra?"

"Exactly, but no money."

"They probably took it; but back to the purse, did you notice the brand of lip gloss?" I paused for dramatics. "It's high end, not dollar store gloss. This woman was way out of her 'neighborhood'." I air quoted neighborhood.

"True, we ran her ID. She lives in an affluent area uptown."

"I'm not surprised. I knew she didn't fit in here." What about the gum?

"It's gum." Tanner shrugged.

"You wouldn't know this, but people who are close to being possessed have rancid Hell breath! She would be very aware of this, thus the multiple packs of gum and wrappers in the purse. We women don't carry around that much gum, but it's pretty typical for the damned."

"The damned?" Tanner cocked an eyebrow. "Is that what you call it?"

"It's what it's called, yes. I can help them if I can get to them before something like this happens." I rubbed my forehead; the headache was raging. "I wasn't fast enough."

"How do you know she was possessed?"

"I don't think she was—yet," I paused. "She was marked, and that I am sure of. You must understand the Devil is tricky; he doesn't just possess people all the time. It's always for some bigger purpose. Not everyone is possessed; sometimes, people are just influenced."

"What do you mean?"

"I mean the power of the evil one can make even the strongest people throw out all their values and do unspeakable things, like a man who kills his wife and kids," I explained, and Tanner didn't say anything. But I could almost see the wheels working in his mind. I wasn't sure if he believed me or not; in the end, it really didn't matter if he believed me. I knew what was true.

"I should have seen the signs in Emily before I lost her," I said and sat up on the side of the bed.

"I haven't known you long, but I'm sure you did what you could." Tanner sat next to me, wrapping one arm around my shoulders. He was warm. I stared into his dark eyes and wondered how much of this concern was real and how much was just as he put it, his job.

"I'm fine." I shrugged off his arm and stood up, pacing the small room. I rubbed my hands together, checking the scrapes from falling. "What do you know about this epidemic?" I wanted to stay on topic, and having his arm around me was not helping me stay on task.

"Not much. In this area of town, there have been ten, now eleven, deaths by overdose. We can't be sure, but I suspect the concoction of fentanyl and cocaine to be found in Emily, as it was in the others. A serial poisoner always has a formula they like to use. A recipe they are comfortable with."

"Emily disappeared off Clark Street." I pulled out my computer and fired up the search engine.

Tanner smiled wide. "You do use technology."

"Just a little. I need something, but you can't trace this like you can a phone." I flipped the screen over to tablet mode and zoomed into the topographic image of Phoenix, specifically Clark Street. "Here is where they took her." I pointed on the screen. "Here is the motel where they found her body." My finger moved across the screen. "The others?"

Tanner leaned over my shoulder. "Here, here, and here," he said as his finger made a circle around the motel.

"We're in the center; this motel is the center of the killings."

"Yes." Tanner cocked his head. "Why did you pick this place to stay?"

Heat filled my face. "Are you insinuating something, Agent?"

"No, not yet," he paused. "It's just a coincidence that you came upon this deadly situation and then are the only person to see Emily abducted."

"Nothing is a coincidence," I said and shut down the laptop. "I'm here for a reason; there are powers at work that you wouldn't and couldn't understand." I rubbed my forehead and sat back down on the bed. "And, by the way, I do not appreciate your insinuation. I didn't have anything to do with Emily being taken. I have told you over and over—I help people!" I gritted my teeth; he was an exasperating man.

"Okay, okay." He raised his hands in defeat. "I have to look at every angle." He leaned toward me. "I'm sorry if I upset you." He smiled and extended one hand. "Friends?"

I took his hand. "Friends." We held hands for a moment; I was the first to pull away.

SEVEN

"Let's go get some food." I stood and grabbed my bag. I was out the door before he could say anything.

Tanner hurried behind me. I was usually running from the FBI, not waiting for them to catch up.

We walked across the street to the diner. Entering, the usual bell dinged. The waitress from the night before looked up from the kitchen. "Hola! Seat yourself. Gracias!" She hollered across the empty diner. I led Tanner to the exact booth I had sat in the day before.

"This is where I saw her. Emily came in and sat at the third stool at the breakfast bar. I could tell she was high, but I could also tell she wasn't a typical junkie, if there is such a thing anymore."

"I've seen every version of addiction; they come in all packages," Tanner said.

"Well, this package was pretty and way out of her element." I eyeballed the stool where she sat, alive, a little over twelve hours ago. "I should have done more."

Tanner reached across the table, taking my hand. "Not everyone is savable."

I slid my hand away. "I will never believe that. I will always fight for them."

"Good. I'm glad you and I are on the same page; I was just testing you."

"Stop with the testing; you make my head spin with the good cop bad cop routine. Just be you. It's exhausting, and I need coffee."

"Deal," Tanner said and motioned for the waitress. "Two coffees, please."

Rosa hurried over with two white mugs and a silver pot of coffee. "Here's some cream and sugar; what else can I get you?" Rosa asked.

"I'll have some hash browns and pancakes." I did love their hash browns.

"I will have a burger, medium, with fries." As Tanner ordered, Rosa nodded and threw him a wink. He smiled at her, his dimples showing, and I swear I saw his cheeks flush. A pang of jealousy rose in me, but I quickly squashed the thought.

"What else do you know about this serial poisoner?" I asked, taking the focus off Rosa. I was sure she had enough attention. I took a sip of coffee.

Tanner stopped staring at Rosa and regarded me. "Not much. It's still in the beginning of the case. You know what I know," he said and took a gulp of coffee.

The door dinged again, and we both glanced up to see a scruffy man in khaki shorts and a dirty, gray t-shirt shuffle into the diner. He sat at the third seat on the breakfast bar. I eyed him carefully, watching his movements and analyzing his every twitch and turn.

"I know him. He was here last night, too. He sat next to Emily; they didn't seem to know each other, but it's odd he's here again." I said a few prayers, and my palms began to tingle. I put my hands under the table.

"Maybe just a local, but certainly someone to look into." Tanner turned to study the man.

I needed to know more about that guy. Tanner tried to grab my arm as I got up from the booth. I dogged his grasp, walked over to the breakfast bar, and sat down. "Hey," I said to the guy.

He looked over at me and kept fidgeting with a straw wrapper.

"How ya doing?" I asked.

"I ain't got no money, so you can go look for

another mark," he said, cupping his coffee mug.

"Oh! No, not looking for anything. I am a friend of Emily's. Do you know her?"

If he did know her, he would have at least known her name.

"No, I don't know no Emily, but my brain isn't what it used to be. I can't remember names too good." He rubbed his forehead.

"You were here last night, right?"

"Yeah, I'm here every night." He nodded to Rosa. "She gives me the expired foods; she is good to us."

"That's nice." I glanced over my shoulder. Tanner was intently staring at us. "You want to join us? I will buy some fresh food."

"Why?" He gave me a puzzled look.

"Just because, come on!" I took him by the arm and led him to the booth where Tanner sat.

"This is Tanner."

Tanner stuck out his hand to shake.

"Kevin," he said and haphazardly shook Tanner's hand as he slid into the booth next to me.

"Nice to meet you, Kevin. You live around here?" Tanner asked.

"Yeah, well, sort of." Kevin glanced out the window and searched up and down the street, rubbing his hands together vigorously. "You two ask a lot of questions." Kevin turned to Tanner. "You don't look like the people around here. You look like a cop. You a cop?"

"Yep," Tanner said quickly, and I kicked him under the table. Everyone knew the last thing you did was give away that you were a freaking cop!

Kevin wiggled in his seat, obviously uncomfortable.

"I'm not here to bother you or anyone. I just want to ask some questions about Emily, the girl they found dead this morning. Lavive said you and she talked last night. I need to know what you said to each other."

"No, we didn't talk; she was just here. I did notice her. She was real pretty and smelled good," he admitted. "I was gonna say something; but she left really fast, and I didn't get a chance."

"So, you haven't seen her around here before?" I interjected.

"No, if she was hanging out here, she was new. I know all the usual people in this neighborhood." Kevin didn't meet our eyes.

Rosa brought over plates of food for all of us. I saw Tanner straighten in his booth, puffing out his chest, when she set his plate down. She smiled and gave me a wink. I had to admit; she was pretty. I could see why every man fell all over themselves, like Tanner was; but it didn't settle well with me. Was I jealous of the waitress? I shook my head at the thought.

We ate in silence, as I refocused on the hundreds

of questions zooming through my brain. Why was Emily in this part of town? Who did she know? Who was she meeting? Why here? Why now? I didn't know any of the answers, but at the very least, the food helped my headache. I looked to my right; my guardian angel floated close. His face seemed a bit strange, his light was dimmer, as if concerned or upset. A tiny alarm went off inside me. Something was off.

The door dinged, and all three of us surveyed the entrance to see two guys walk into the diner. It was difficult to tell which was more disheveled than the other. One was really tall, at least six-seven; the other was starkly short in comparison. They looked over at us, and the tall one instantly made me uncomfortable; his stare was intense and unnerving. The air in the diner had changed. Sulfur permeated the room.

"Hey." Kevin nodded at the two men and got up from the table. He turned to Tanner and me. "Thanks for the food, but I gotta go." He started toward the guys but then turned back to me. "That girl didn't hang with us. I know that much. Sorry she died, but people die around here all the time."

We watched Kevin walk away. The group fist-bumped each other and muttered to themselves. The tall guy gazed at me again. I sipped my coffee but never took my eyes off the group.

"Do you smell that?" Tanner asked. "Smells like

rotten eggs."

"Yeah, I do." I searched the group for some sign of an attachment to a drug demon, black smoke or black eyes, either would alarm me to the one emanating the sulfur smell. "It's them; it's the demon. It's attached to one of them."

"What? Where?" Tanner examined the group.

"You can't see what I see, Tanner. I will let you know if there is anything."

"I'll just go talk to those punks; one of them will know something that's going on around here." Tanner started to stand up.

"No!" I threw my hands up.

"Excuse me!" Tanner's eyebrows raised.

I exhaled, calming my tone. "I've been doing this for years, and sometimes, you just wait. This is a tricky demon, a smart one, a higher-level demon. We need to draw it out; it's the way it works. It hides in someone. So, it has to show itself to be taken down. Remember, it's not a person; it's a demon." I eyed Tanner and pointed at him to take a seat. "This is my specialty."

"Fine," he said and settled back down into the booth.

The men crowded around the breakfast bar area, and Rosa passed out coffee. She came over to the table where we sat and refreshed our cups.

"¿Cómo estás? How are you doing?" Rosa asked and cleared the empty plates.

"Yeah, just fine. Thank you, Rosa," I said without looking at her. The door dinged again.

"What would we do without that door announcing every Tom, Dick, and Harry who walks in here?" Tanner said with a snarky tone.

I rolled my eyes. "Actually do your job, investigate and pay attention?" A cop walked into the diner—not just any cop though. It was Officer Matthews.

My guardian angel appeared and floated right in front of me, obstructing my view of the group of men and the cop. I peered around him, but he didn't move; I could see the men through the angel, but not as clearly. I motioned for him to move. He didn't. I wiggled over toward the window to get a better look at the group. I saw Matthews walking toward us.

"Isn't that the same cop?" Tanner asked

"Yeah, that's him," I whispered.

"Hello again, Ms. Willot, Agent O'Connely." Matthews addressed us formally, shaking hands with Tanner and myself. I was distracted watching the group of men at the bar.

"Please, sit with us." Tanner motioned for Matthews to join us.

I gave Tanner an annoyed look, but then I saw it! A thin ribbon of smoke snuck into the dining room, under the front door just like last night, and intertwined with the group of men. It moved exactly as it had with Emily. I wasn't going to lose it again. I jumped up from the booth, went around Matthews, and headed toward the men.

"Where are you going?" Tanner asked.

I waved off Tanner and kept my eyes on the smoke. I watched the ribbon of black smoke wind around the legs of the men. It split like tree limbs and intertwined itself with the group. It moved with swiftness I hadn't seen before. By the time, I was a foot away from Kevin, the entire group suddenly stopped talking, froze for a moment, and then all rushed outside. The smoke dissipated, as it moved toward the door. Rushing outside behind them, I followed, staying a few feet back.

Some man grabbed my arm and pulled me toward him. "What are you doing?" I snapped. "I have to follow them."

"You need to be careful," said Officer Matthews.

Shocked that it wasn't Tanner interfering this time, it took me a few moments to pull my arm from his grasp.

"Is there a problem?" Tanner asked as he reached us.

"No!" I glared at Matthews and rushed to the corner. Searching up and down the street, I caught a glimpse of one of the men rounding another corner a block away. *They move fast*, I thought. "Dammit!" I took off down the block.

"What is happening?" Tanner yelled as he stood

at the diner door.

Ignoring him, I rounded the corner and scanned the street, expecting to see the group of guys. But instead, there was nothing, not a soul in sight. The slight smell of sulfur lingered in the air. I scanned the street, frantically, up and down, side to side. As I moved quickly, I briefly stopped at store windows and scrutinized alleys. They were nowhere to be found. "Shit!" I stomped my foot.

"What?" Tanner asked breathlessly, catching up to me. "Where are they?"

"Not here, Tanner!" I snapped back, rolled my eyes, and turned away from him. He was slowing me down, taking my attention off what I was here to do. "Shit!" I said again, kicking a rock.

"We will find them; they can't just disappear," Tanner said, walking down the street and looking around the buildings.

"You!" I caught up to him and poked his chest. "This is your fault! I should have known better than to pseudo team up with you or anyone! This is life or death, and you slow me down! I can't work like this." I hurried a few feet away from him, but then turned back. "This." I motioned between myself and him. "This, whatever this is, is over!" I stormed off.

As I rushed away, I could feel Tanner's eyes on me. I huffed and took a left down an alley just to get out of his eyesight. I couldn't believe where I'd

let this get to. I was the one in charge of demon
hunting! Not a dimple-cheeked FBI agent. I balled
my fists and kicked a can down the alley. It
skidded across the asphalt and landed against a
dumpster. I watched it land in a dirty puddle of
rancid water. The alley was damp and hidden in
the shadows of the midmorning sun. A chill ran up
my spine.

A clang of metal on metal perked me right up,
and I looked around. "Tanner?" Was he ever going
to leave me alone?

"No, not the cop," a male voice said, his deep
voice reverberating off the brick buildings. I froze
as the alarm bells were going off in my head. I
began to say the Our Father prayer and rubbed my
hands together. The power formed, as wisps of
light radiated from my palms. I swung my
shoulder bag around and pulled out my mace and
holy water. I'd need one or the other and on a
really bad day, both.

"Lavive," the voice sang. "You look so pretty
today."

I tightened my grip on the holy water and
mace.

EIGHT

"What do you want?" I said in the most demanding voice I could muster.

"You, silly." The sound of metal dragging across the asphalt filled the alleyway. "I'm going to do so many bad things to you."

"Sorry, buddy, I am not in the mood!" I squeezed the container of mace and clicked off the safety lever. I might have had supernatural gifts of the Spirit, but mace still brought down the average bad guy. I prayed to St. Michael and said a Hail Mary. My palms engulfed in light. "Come on out and show yourself!" I demanded.

"Hi!" The voice behind me made me jump. I turned and crouched down in a fighting position, thrusting forward my glowing hands.

"Ohhhhhh, look at this!" He laughed a deep guttural laugh.

I sprayed the mace. It was a direct hit! He let out a loud holler and fell to the ground. Throwing the mace to the side, I held my hands out, illuminating the area.

"Kevin!" I blinked a few times. "What are you doing, Kevin?"

He wiped his eyes and stood back up. His face was red. He took his shirt and raised it to wipe the mace from his eyes.

"That hurt!" he yelled and stared at me; his eyes were black. The area was filled with the smell of sulfur.

"It usually does," I said and took my stance with my palms outward.

Kevin cocked his head to one side. "You know, I watched you yesterday and today. I wanted you so bad, Lavive. I could just grab those long, white dreads and wrap them around my fists." He reached out for me, but I jumped backward.

"This isn't you, Kevin. You have to fight this." I tried to talk past the demon, straight to Kevin. I knew he was in there somewhere. I looked closer in his eyes. They did not appear fully black; they still had a pin-size white light shining through. "You have a choice; you can choose to fight this." I tried to negotiate, but really, I was just distracting him.

"But this is good. I like this feeling, and that Emily girl liked it, too."

My mind spun. "Was that you in the black car? Did you take her? Are you the one killing these people?"

He let out another guttural laugh. "What do you think, Deliverer?"

"What did you do to Emily?" I asked the demon inside Kevin.

"Nothing she didn't want. We partied is all." Kevin smiled. "She tasted like money and strawberry lip gloss." He rubbed his lips with his thumb. "I wonder what you will taste like."

"Well, you will never find out." I lunged at him and grabbed his face with both hands. He fell to his knees, as my power flowed out of me and into him. He moaned and thrashed, but I kept hold of him. I prayed the deliverance prayers in the tongue of angels. Focusing on the Holy Spirit I could feel pulse through me, I felt the heat of the Trinity, the power of goodness, of God.

"Stop," Kevin croaked, as I continued to pray.

"What is your name, demon?"

"Kevin."

"No, what is your name, demon!" I demanded.

Kevin contorted and fell fully to the ground. I straddled his chest, my hands never leaving his face. The light radiating from my palms showed the pain and agony of the demon. I couldn't help but feel good knowing I was causing that demon some discomfort. It was one of the benefits of this job, at least I got to see evil lose.

Kevin arched his back and twisted; I almost fell off but held on and continued to pray. "Your name!" I yelled.

"Lust," it hissed.

"In the name of Jesus Christ, I cast out the demon of Lust from this man. Where His name is invoked, you cannot stay." I continued to pray the deliverance prayers, my hands numb with the power of the Spirit.

Kevin thrashed his head back and forth. I held on and prayed as hard as I could.

My hands burned bright white. I knew this part was the worst of it. "Leave, demon, you are no longer welcome here." I traced a cross on his forehead with holy water.

Kevin arched back, his mouth agape, as the ribbon of black smoke crept out of his throat. It wound its way up and into a twister of blackness, a mass above us. As the tail of the smoke left Kevin, he instantly relaxed and crashed back onto the ground, his body like a ragdoll. His head fell to one side. I watched the demon smoke hover a few feet above us. "Go back to Hell!" I yelled and threw holy water on the smoke. It sizzled and dissipated into nothingness. I took note that it was obviously a lower-level demon; it couldn't even manifest into human form.

The alley was still. I knelt by Kevin and cradled his head in my lap. "You will be okay," I assured him as the light in my palms dimmed. I let out a loud exhale. *That one wasn't too bad*, I thought. It could have been worse. I'd had worse.

"What? What is happening?" Kevin opened his eyes and blinked a few times. "My eyes are on fire," he said, noticing the mace canister I'd thrown aside. "Did you mace me?" He rubbed his eyes and sat up.

"Sorry about that," I said, standing up. "You were kind of out of control. Do you remember anything?"

"No." Kevin shook his head. "I was in the diner and then here." He squinted and glanced around the alley. "What happened?" he asked as he stood.

I wondered what I should tell him. Most people who did remember being under the influence of a demon really didn't want to remember anything. It was a blessing that he didn't.

"I'm not sure," I lied. "Maybe someone slipped you something? You were acting weird, and I had to mace you. "

Kevin rubbed his eyes and flinched. I grabbed a bottle of tap water from my bag and put a few drops of holy water in it, handing it to Kevin. "Sorry again about that, but it must have worked to get you to wake up."

He took the water and poured it on his eyes, rubbing the mace off his face. That was one way of blessing him without it getting weird.

"Yeah, but I feel ok now, except for my eyes." He blinked a few times and sniffed.

"Lavive!" Tanner yelled from the end of the alley. Kevin and I turned to see him barreling down the alley like a linebacker. I was instantly worried for Kevin.

I jumped in front of him and held my hands up; luckily, they had stopped glowing. I thought Tanner would have freaked out. "Tanner, it's fine; we are fine."

Tanner stopped a few feet away. He looked like he was about to kick both of our asses.

"We were just talking—"

"Really?" Tanner motioned toward Kevin, wiping his face again.

"Okay, I had to mace him—"

Tanner advanced; I put my hands on his chest. "It's fine now," I said intently and looked him in the eye. "I promise."

"Let's go." Tanner wrapped his large arm around my waist and pulled me away from Kevin.

"I got this," I said with force and pushed out of his arms. The last thing I needed was Tanner getting possessive. I certainly wasn't anyone's property. "You can relax."

"Fine." Tanner's jaw tightened and stood to the

side.

We said goodbye to Kevin, and I was grateful that I was able to help him with his lust demon, although I was surprised it wasn't the drug demon. Doubt crept in; maybe I was wrong about the higher-level demon. But I was never usually wrong. I guessed there was a first time for everything.

"What happened with Kevin?" Tanner asked, as we almost got to the motel. We were about fifty feet from my room.

I tried to avoid the truth. "It was nothing. I think he must have been slipped some drug or something and went crazy." I shrugged my shoulders.

"Did he hurt you?"

Tanner's jaw was tight, like anger seethed through him.

"No, he didn't hurt me." I put my hand on Tanner's chest. "I'm really ok; I promise."

He put his hand on mine and squeezed. Some part of me wanted to hold him tightly until he believed me; another part of me was just pissed that he didn't believe me!

"You are exhausting," I said and pulled my hand back.

He actually laughed, like he could hear my thoughts.

I rolled my eyes. "I'm going back to bed; stalk

me later." I winked at Tanner before turning and opening my door.

I closed the door behind me a smile plastered on my face. My angel floated near the bed. His face ever so beautiful, and his light had returned to normal, which was good to see.

"Where were you?" My smiled faded quickly, and I placed my hands on my hips. "I was fighting a demon in an alley and no angel anywhere." I flung my red leather jacket and cross-body bag on the bed. I pointed to my angel. "I'm taking a shower; you stay here."

I didn't know why I fought with my angel; he never fought back. It was the human in me that wanted answers. Deep down, I knew there were reasons my angel wouldn't interfere, free will and all that business. Life was carefully orchestrated, but it was aggravating.

The shower was hot, and I let it pour over my face. My life had become so complicated in the past few days. I needed to get it back under some sort of control. My angel being weird, lighting up and not showing when I needed it. Plus, Tanner wouldn't leave me alone, and the crazy thing was I wasn't sure if I wanted him to. It was all too much drama. I mean, damn, I was already fighting demons; throw in a hot guy with a hotter temper and a stubborn guardian angel? I was at my limit.

I couldn't even enjoy the shower; I was too

frustrated. On one hand, Kevin was freed and safe, which was awesome; on the other, I had to deal with my angel and Tanner. Not to mention, I had a nagging feeling in the pit of my stomach that the demon from Kevin wasn't the demon I was hunting. I was hunting a higher-level drug demon; the lust demon in Kevin was way too easy to banish.

After drying off and dressing in some clean pajamas, I left the small bathroom and went back into the bedroom; my angel was in the exact same place. "Good to see you can listen—sometimes."

I beheld my angel and felt the calming warmth flow from him. "I know," I said and sighed. "I'm sure you were doing what you needed to do to help me." I half-smiled. "Thank you, even if it is extremely aggravating. Thank you." I sat on the bed, my hair still wrapped in a towel.

The angel lifted its translucent hand and gently stroked my cheek. He touched me again! Why? I was so confused with the changes in my angel. I was unnerved but was taken out of my thoughts and pulled into the feeling of his touch. It felt as if a cloud could come and hold me. I closed my eyes and enjoyed the rare feeling of my angel's touch. My body relaxed and felt as if I was floating. It was blissful, actually blissful. There was no room for questions or concerns; there was nothing but love and light. All other issues, Kevin, Tanner,

Matthews — they all melted into the night, as I was peacefully lulled to sleep.

NINE

A knock at the door woke me from a heavenly sleep. "What?" I hollered from the bed. Full knowing the only person that would be knocking was Tanner.

"Lavive, it's Tanner."

I rolled over in bed and cocooned myself in the blankets.

"Go away," I yelled from under the covers.

"Lavive, open the door; it's important." Tanner's tone was alarming. He wasn't his normal self; there was a sense of urgency in his voice. The hair on my arms stood on end.

"Shit," I muffled as I unwrapped from the tornado of blankets and sheets. Stumbling out of bed, I crossed the small room and unlocked the door. Pulling it open, Tanner stood, freshly showered and dressed in black jeans and a black shirt with a tan man-bag hung at his hip; his hair was still wet. His face was drawn into a tense stare.

"What?" I asked, "What happened?"

"Kevin." Tanner's eyes fell to the ground. "Kevin's body was found a block away, another overdose."

"What?" I felt my knees weaken and slowly turned away from Tanner to sit on the bed. I glanced up at him, half-believing I hadn't heard him correctly. "What?" I asked again.

"I'm so sorry, Lavive. We found him about thirty minutes ago."

I replayed the morning in my mind. I had freed him of the lust demon attachment. He was safe, at least I had thought so. I checked the clock. I had only been asleep three hours; that wasn't even enough time for a demon to kill! Was it? A wave of sadness crashed over me. I had failed; somehow, I had failed him.

"I've only failed one other time this badly." My eyes stung, and I let my head hang.

"Do you want to talk about it?"

I shook my head no; I didn't like to remember my failures.

Tanner sat next to me and wrapped his arm around my shoulder. I pressed into him and let him comfort me. Burrowing my face in the crook of his neck, I breathed in his scent. The shock of Kevin's death was overwhelming. I ran through the morning again and again, plus everything I knew about demons. What the hell!

I pushed down the sadness and let my frustration take over. "Ugh," I said and stood up, leaving Tanner sitting on the bed. "As I lay here sleeping, Kevin dies! Great defender, my ass!" I paced the small room, giving my angel the side-eye. I wasn't so grateful for his help at that moment. "I don't know what I could have done, but we shouldn't have left Kevin."

Thinking back, I realized that Tanner had showed up after I thought I had freed Kevin from the lust demon.

"You can't blame yourself," Tanner said.

My eyes widened. "I don't blame myself! I blame YOU!" I snapped. "I let this happen on my watch, mine!" I stormed the room and balled my fists, tears stung my eyes, but I wasn't about to cry. "All these distractions have kept me from my job!" I stopped and looked at Tanner in the eyes. "You," I said with disdain. "You kept me from saving him. Since the moment I met you, all you have done is slow me down." I glared. "I don't need you to help me; I am better off without you."

Tanner stood and squared his chest.

I decided that this felt right, what I was saying

was right. If I worked alone, kept everyone out, I could concentrate on the demons and not the handsome FBI agent. "I want you out, not just this room, but this town, my life, all of it. Erase the files you may have on me; you know I'm not a threat to national security. Just go, Tanner. Leave me. I have work to do, and you just get in the way!"

"What the hell are you talking about, Lavive? I have only helped you. I have listened to your crazy antics, and I have given you the benefit of the doubt. If anything, you should be thanking me!"

"Thanking you?" I scoffed.

"Yes, I could have taken you in way back in Chicago, but I didn't."

"Oh, thank you so much! You are too sweet." I narrowed my eyes at him.

Tanner stood stone-faced. "Fine." He pulled a manila folder out of the bag and threw it on the bed. "Here is your file; we are done here." Tanner turned and left without another word.

Watching the door close behind him, the thought crossed my mind to stop him; I almost called his name. My hand covered my mouth; I wouldn't stop him.

I sat on the side of the bed, getting my head straight. I needed to focus, to center myself. Too many distractions had caused me to mess up, and I couldn't do it again. I grabbed my rosary from the nightstand and started praying. I'd been disconnected, and time of prayer was essential to keep me focused and sharp.

Finishing the 10th decade of the Rosary, I said the St. Michael, the archangel prayer, and picked up my Bible. Closing my eyes, I flipped through the pages. This was something my priest friend taught me years ago.

"Flip until the Holy Spirit stops you; there you will find the message needed."

I stopped and read the page.

Matthew 7:15:

"Beware of false prophets, which come to you in sheep's clothing, but inwardly they are ravening wolves."

I pondered the Bible verse. Who was the wolf? Tanner? He'd been the only other new player in my life. I'd opened up to him; maybe he was the wolf. It fit what the Devil did—someone got close to you with lies and trickery, and then they showed their true colors. But Tanner hadn't done anything too bad. Yes, he was a pain in my ass, but he seemed to genuinely care about helping and getting to the bottom of the deaths. Was it all a ruse, a lie, some smokescreen of evil that I couldn't see through?

Getting up and dressed, I needed to get air, to walk, to think. Opening the motel door, I ran straight into Officer Mathews.

"Whoa!" I said and raised my hands. "What are you doing here?"

"Well, good evening to you, Ms. Willot. I was coming to talk with you about Kevin Adams, the man that we found today. You talked to him this morning at the diner; you shared a meal."

"Yes." I shut the door behind me and locked it. "Kevin did have a meal with me earlier; he's a nice guy." I turned to look at Matthews. "*Was* a nice guy." I corrected.

Matthews's eyes dropped. He was young, not even thirty. His small frame was hidden under the bulletproof vest, uniform, and all the necessary attachments. He held a pad of paper in one hand and fidgeted with a pen in the other.

"What can I help you with?" I asked nicely. I'd learned to comply when necessary, not like with Tanner. With him, I was full-scale crazy.

"What were you doing with him this morning?"

"Eating."

"What else?" He probed with his head down, taking notes.

"Talking," I said.

"I know you're new around here. What were you doing with a known drug addict in this part of town?"

"This is where I'm staying for the time being. I don't plan on being here long."

"Where's Special Agent O'Connely?"

"I honestly don't know where he is." I thought of our fight earlier and pushing Tanner away. "I'm sure you can find him; you're a cop after all. I'm done with him." I began walking away from the motel toward the diner. "I need coffee; you want some?" I pointed to the Waffle House.

Matthews nodded, and we walked in silence.

The familiar ding of the doorbell sounded our arrival, as we entered the small diner. The beautiful black man was back in his same booth, sipping on a coffee mug. A super-strong smell of onions and coffee invaded my senses. *A strange combination*, I thought. We sat in the same booth. I viewed the spot where Kevin sat less than twelve hours ago — alive. Pulling my dreadlocks up in a messy bun and fidgeting in my seat fought back the emotions that I would only let out when alone.

"Hola!" Rosa sang from the kitchen. "I'll be right there with some coffee. Just finishing chopping these dang onions."

"Thanks, Rosa!" I yelled back.

"Did Kevin say anything to you about where he was going or who he was meeting?" Matthews studied me and then glanced down at his notepad. He was all business, which was fine with me. The fewer emotions, the better.

"No," I said and clasped my hands together. "He didn't say anything that will help you find the serial poisoner."

Matthews straightened his back; his eyes widened. "I didn't, I—" He stuttered.

I held up a hand to stop him. "I know all about what is happening around here. I was just talking with Kevin about Emily. Trying to see if they knew each other or hung around the same people. We want the same thing, Matthews. I don't want to see anyone else die either. But I don't know anything." I wrung my hands together, remembering the deliverance of the lust demon.

"Buenos días," Rosa greeted us and poured coffee for me.

"Orange juice please." Mathews covered his mug with his hand as Rosa was about to pour him a cup.

I was grateful for the distraction even if Rosa smelled like a fresh-cut pile of onions.

"Good morning, Rosa," I said and looked up at her, immediately confused. She was wearing big sunglasses, the kind that people wear after laser eye surgery. "What's with the glasses? Are you okay?"

"Yes, dear, it's just those onions, whew! They really get to my eyes. These help keep out the juices." She laughed and adjusted her glasses.

I smiled and laughed with her.

"I'll get your orange juice and be right back," Rosa said and went back to the kitchen.

I raised my coffee and nodded to Matthews with a fake cheers, then took a few gulps of coffee. Shivers ran down my spine; the hairs on my arms stood on end. The mug in my hand slipped, spilling coffee onto the table. I tried to find the cause of my alarm, but it was just Rosa, Matthews and the lone black man in the diner. My guardian angel floated near the front door, the tips of his wings turning a slight pink.

TEN

I shivered as the icy tendrils of the evil force crawled across my skin like a spider through honey. The world seemed to tilt on its side. My stomach turned.

"Are you ok?" Matthews waved his hand in front of my face.

I refocused on him and squinted. "Yes." I bit my bottom lip and searched his face for any sign of the demon. His eyes were a deep blue and the whites showed signs of a lack of sleep, not the tell-tale blackness of the damned. "Dammit," I grunted and pushed back from the table, crawling out of the booth. I needed to find the person the demon was attached to and expel it before it killed any more people.

Unfortunately for me, this one was very good at hiding. I could feel the evil grow, as I moved toward the door, like an unseen mountain I was trying to climb. Sweat trickled down my back when I reached the door handle. While I opened the door, the ring of the bell echoed in my brain. The world spun like a crazy carnival ride. Whatever this demon was, it was stronger than I had predicted. Sliding down the glass door, I clenched my eyes shut and prayed.

"What is happening?" Matthews crossed the small diner and was at my side before I hit the ground.

"It's fine," I slurred.

"This doesn't look fine! I'm calling this in."

"She doesn't look so good. No bueno!" Rosa said as she leaned over the diner breakfast bar.

"Nooooooo," I whispered.

The world got dark, and I passed out on the diner floor.

A jarring thud brought me back. I opened my eyes to see the roof of an ambulance, as they wheeled me in. "I am fine." I mouthed, but no one heard or paid any attention to me. There was one EMT checking me over, just like I'd seen them do so many times at all the demonic events I'd witnessed.

Some demon hunter, I thought, *I can't even keep*

upright!

"Lavive!" Tanner's voice carried a tone of concern and urgency. "Lavive! Are you okay?"

I raised a hand.

He crawled into the already cramped ambulance and muscled his way past the EMT to be at my head. He brushed the hair from my face. "You really need to get it together. I can't worry about you this much. I thought you were the tough one," he said and stroked my cheek.

"Sir, we are heading to the hospital. Please, excuse me," the EMT said.

Ignoring her, Tanner stared into my eyes and bent toward my face. My heart pounded and throat dried. He kissed me gently on the forehead.

"I'm right here with you." He was inches from me, and I could feel his heat.

I couldn't help but smile.

"Please, lift me up," I asked.

The EMT tilted up the gurney. I was able to see out the back of the open ambulance doors. A small group had formed right outside; Matthews looked concerned, and Rosa was there, along with a few other gawkers.

"Take care," Matthews waved.

"Yeah, you take care, señorita." Rosa waved with one hand and pulled down her big, black sunglasses with the other.

My heart skipped a beat, as adrenaline rushed

through my system. My mouth gaped open. I stared into the deep black pools of Rosa's eyes. It. Was. Her.

I blinked wildly while trying to wrap my head around what I was seeing. The doors of the ambulance suddenly slammed shut, and the outside world was cut off.

"No!" I reached out for the door.

Tanner held me down.

"Let me go! You don't understand!"

"Lavive, you have to get some rest; they are trying to figure out what happened."

Tanner tried to calm me, but I fought him. He didn't know what I knew. Now that the demon had shown itself, my time was limited to getting it expelled. It could hop from Rosa to another vessel if it wanted; demons could bilocate, like angels. They could do a lot of things normal people didn't know about. Tanner might be a smart man; but on this subject, he was completely ignorant, and I wasn't even sure if he believed me.

I took Tanner's face in my hands. "Listen to me, you have to go back and watch Rosa. It's her!"

"What's her?"

"She is the one with the demon attachment; she's the one influencing the others to take the drugs that are killing them. She is the serial poisoner. She may be too far gone to even know what she is doing at this point, but you have to watch her until I get out of here and can get back to the diner."

"Rest, Lavive, there is time to investigate Rosa. But I don't think that sweet Mexican flower has anything to do with the street addicts dying."

"Listen to me!" I begged as the ambulance drove off.

I collapsed back onto the gurney; my thoughts were fuzzy, and eyelids suddenly very heavy. "You have to listen. You have to watch her. . ." I trailed off.

Waking up, I blinked in rhythm with the heart monitor. I was in a hospital emergency room. It was small and sparse; each bed separated by blue curtains. My head pounded, as I lifted myself off the pillow. Massaging my temples, I ran through the night's events. I needed to get to Tanner and to Rosa. The memory of Rosa's eyes flashed, and I shivered.

How did I miss the signs that the demon was in Rosa? There weren't the obvious signs that are normally accompanied by the damned, like speaking in different voices or dialects. I had smelled the sulfur and saw the black ribbon, but it wasn't near her, which was weird. Rosa had seemed as normal as anyone.

I carefully stood and stretched my legs; there must have been something I should have seen sooner. No other demon I'd ever encountered was that good at hiding, and why did it show itself at that moment? What was it planning?

My breath caught in my throat. "Dammit," I whispered. I knew why it revealed itself; it was near its final target. It was close to finishing the goal, whatever that was. Before, in Chicago, it had been a mass shooting or a fire or some other large casualty situation. What was this one planning?

I searched for my shoes. This demon wasn't flashy; its tactics were stealthier. What did it want?

I found my clothes tucked in a clear bag on the chair. I changed out of the hospital gown. I took a deep breath and pulled out the IV. The buzzers started going off.

"What are you doing?" Tanner asked from the opened curtain.

I looked up at him. "We have to get to Rosa. There is something big going to happen. I don't know what it is yet, but I know it has to do with her." I put my shoes on. "Let's go," I said and walked past Tanner.

"What the actual Hell, Lavive?" Tanner said as he hurried to pace me. "There is nothing in or possessing Rosa. While they were admitting you, I went back and talked to her for a bit. She is just a nice girl working in a tiny diner, making a living! She isn't damned or whatever you call it." His tone was flippant.

I would have put him in his place if it wasn't

dire that I get to Rosa. Tanner and his attitude would have to wait until I had more time, but I'd come back to his trust issues and teach him a thing or two about the damned.

"Where is your car?" I asked. I had no idea where I was or how to get back to the diner.

"Miss, you need to come back to the bed and lie down." A nurse was at my side. "The doctor hasn't discharged you yet; you will need to wait until he does in order to leave."

Tanner smiled. He didn't say anything, just waved his hand toward the hospital bed I had been in.

I looked at the nurse and then at Tanner. "Dammit, Tanner!" I whined as I threw my head back and balled my fists. I needed him at this moment. I hated it, but I needed him. I stormed back and threw myself on the bed like a toddler having a temper tantrum.

"Are you done?" Tanner asked as he walked through the curtains.

"Not even a little," I said and sat up. "Why are you doing this? You know I need your help to get back to the diner. I'm telling you—this is a matter of life or death. I have to help Rosa and get that demon back to Hell!"

"I know you think you have to do all that, but what you really have to do is rest," Tanner interjected. "Somehow you were drugged with meth; it's what made you pass out in the diner. I haven't figured out who, but the locals are testing everything in the diner."

"Test the coffee; it's all I had," I said, and Tanner nodded, pulling out his phone.

"I'll text Matthews."

I nodded and held my head. I was still a bit queasy from being drugged. Luckily Mathews didn't have the coffee.

"It's past midnight; everyone is sleeping, and so should you." Tanner eyed the pillow.

I rolled my eyes and laid down. I would never admit it, but I was truly exhausted. I knew I couldn't face a powerful demon in my current state, but not doing anything wasn't my style either. Tanner took a seat in the recliner next to the bed. He pulled a cover over himself and smiled. I knew he wasn't leaving.

I turned my back to him and saw my guardian angel floating near the window. I searched his face for some direction on what to do. He was beautiful as always but lacking the human expressions I needed. I considered his wings; they were back to their normal blue translucence, and I exhaled in relief. I really didn't need to also worry about him turning pink or maroon or any other color at the moment. I was still trying to figure out what a guardian angel changing colors meant, but I did know it was bad.

My angel moved toward me; he warmed the air and softened the world, as his light replaced the fear, doubt, and apprehension I held onto.

ELEVEN

Light streamed into the hospital windows; I covered my face with a blanket and heard Tanner stir in the recliner. Immediately, I thought of Rosa and the look of her eyes the night before. The wink she gave me dripped with confidence, and I wanted to make sure to take down that cocky demon—and of course, save Rosa in the process. That was a given.

I stretched and threw the covers off; I was still dressed from my midnight attempt at escaping. I sat and watched Tanner; he was still somewhat asleep, his face lacking any worry. I stared for a few minutes.

"Hey! Wake up," I finally said while putting on

my shoes.

Tanner blinked and sat up, stretching and moaning a soft good morning.

"You said I had to rest; I did. Now, let's get going to find Rosa; I have a lot of work to do." I stood next to Tanner and held his shoulder bag and shoes in my hands. "Let's go." I tossed his bag in his lap and dropped his shoes.

"Fine," Tanner said with a yawn. "But I am stopping for coffee, and you have zero say in the matter!" He slid on his shoes and rubbed his eyes.

I didn't think I would be drinking any coffee for a long while.

Not long after talking to the doctor, who confirmed that I was indeed drugged, we were walking out of the hospital into the parking lot. We drove out of the lot and twenty minutes to the diner and motel. As we exited the highway and turned the corner, I saw the flashing lights of police cars and ambulances.

"Dammit, Tanner!" I slapped him on the arm.

"What? I didn't know anything was happening." He pulled out his phone. "Shit, eight missed messages. I turned it off last night; and you rushed me out. I didn't even check it."

We parked in between two cop cars. My door was open before the car fully stopped. I hustled past the police tape and ignored the calls from officers. My eyes fixed on the diner windows.

Through the glass, I could make out the form of a man slumped over in a booth, my booth.

"Wait!" Tanner yelled, getting my attention. I turned to him. His brow was drawn together, and he bit his lower lip. "Lavive, I talked to the uniforms, it's one of their own. It's Matthews."

"What!" My eyes bulged, and I whipped my head around toward the diner. I took a few steps closer and focused on the form; now, I could make out the outline of Matthew's body. "How?" I asked, fully knowing the answer, but silently prayed it was a shooting or a robbery that had gone bad — something other than Rosa and an overdose.

"Preliminary reports are an overdose, like the others."

"Dammit." My head dropped. I shouldn't have stayed the night at the hospital. I should have warned Matthews. I should have done a million other things, but I hadn't. Guilt covered me like molten lava — thick, painful, and constant. I burned under the weight of the pain.

"I should have done something," I whispered.

He rubbed my back, and we headed toward the motel. I wondered how Rosa's demon had convinced Matthews to do drugs. *A demon can't make anyone do anything; there is always free will,* I thought. I stopped and turned toward the diner. Tanner pulled me away from the Waffle House, but I resisted.

"I need to see him," I said as I wiggled out of his arms. "I have to see Matthews."

Tanner followed behind me, waving off the officers as we got closer. Taking a deep breath before opening the diner door, the waft of onions stung my eyes. Matthews' body was leaning back in the booth, one of his sleeves rolled up with a tourniquet around the bicep and a needle hanging haphazardly from the crook of his arm. I swallowed hard. In front of Matthews was a cup of coffee, a red rose in a clear glass vase, and a plate of hash browns with cheese. I winced.

"I thought you said he died like the others?" I asked Tanner, but my eyes never left the needle in his arm.

"He did." Tanner walked around me to the edge of the booth. "It was a drug overdose."

"I see that!" I pointed to the needle. "But this is not the same! The others were all cocaine laced with fentanyl, inhaled. This is obviously an intravenous overdose."

"Yes, but the drug is the same as the serial poisoner has been using; it matched the composite profile. True, it was liquefied, but the composition was identical."

"Someone could have drugged him!"

"I thought of that; but searching the scene we didn't find anyone's prints on the needle, the table, or anything else."

"But someone could have done it or influenced him. I don't think he did this to himself. This isn't an accidental overdose. This is murder!" I pondered the implications. Taking away free will wasn't something a demon was capable of, so how did this demon convince a strait-laced cop to inject himself with a deadly drug? I'd never seen that level of control. How in the heavens could that happen? Fear rocked through my body. I was fully convinced this wasn't a normal demon; it was the highest level, possibly even the Devil himself.

I froze, as the thought of battling the Devil set in. I stumbled back toward the diner breakfast bar and leaned against the counter.

"What is it?" Tanner asked as he held my shoulders steady.

"This is bad, Tanner. This is really, really bad."

"I know it's upsetting, but we need to focus on finding Rosa and stopping this madness—if she is the serial poisoner. Do you have any ideas on where she could be?"

I shook my head. "They hide. They hide, but she will come out. I need to think, to regroup."

"Okay, I'll take you to your room." Tanner ushered me out of the diner, leaving Matthews and the uneaten cheese hash browns.

We reached the motel room. Tanner unlocked the door and led me in. Sitting on the bed, my shoulders slumped and head hung low.

"It's winning," I whispered. "It's winning."

"Lavive, look at me." Tanner placed his hands on the side of my face. "You had nothing to do with this. Matthews chose—"

"Did he?" I asked and pulled away, wiping my face and taking a few deep breaths. I did my best to compose myself. "I don't know what happened with Matthews, but I'm going to find out. This demon is not going to win!"

"It's not a demon; there are no demons to fight, Lavive. This is just people making bad decisions. There is no big, bad evil at work. You must stop thinking this way. It's making you crazy!" Tanner threw up his hands.

I jerked my head up. "You don't believe me!" I shouted. "After all that I have told you, shown you, what you've actually seen with your own eyes, you still don't believe me?" I gritted my teeth. "I have only been honest; I have shown you the most vulnerable parts of myself, and you still can sit here and call me crazy!" My blood boiled.

"I didn't mean you are crazy, just acting crazy— just a bit." Tanner backpedaled. "You yourself said there was free will. I just don't think there is a big, bad actual demon influencing these people. They are people making bad decisions—nothing else. I am an FBI agent; I have a criminal to find and arrest, not a demon!"

"This is why there is so much evil floating

around. People like you who think you can just use your own will to snap out of it. You are an idiot!" I yelled.

"Hey!" Tanner stood and put up his hand. "Settle down. I'm on your side."

"Are you?" I stood. "Get out," I shouted. My arm shook, as I pointed toward the door.

"Lavive, please," Tanner said softly, but I was already livid. His phone rang, and he pulled it out.

As he talked, I paced the small room.

Hanging up, he looked at me. "Fine, I'll go. But I am leaving because they need me at the scene, not because you're telling me to," he said and turned toward the door. "Stay safe," he whispered before leaving the room.

I grunted and stomped around the room like a five-year-old. Tanner was only hindering my hunt; Matthews died because I wasn't on top of my game. Rosa was possessed, and I didn't even see it or feel it for days! What the actual hell was going on? All my auto-tuned demon gifts were malfunctioning, and I didn't know why.

The charisms I had been given should have been going off like sirens around Rosa. I couldn't figure out why they didn't. The gift of discernment should have warned me about the demon as soon as I was near it. All I could think was that it was good at hiding. My gift of deliverance and speaking in tongues seemed to be working, at least it did on Kevin, even though he ended up dying anyway.

"UGH!" I balled my first and paced the room.

My guardian angel floated near the window, and I glared at him. *He should have been helping me more*, I thought.

If anyone could be pissed at an angel, it was me. "What am I supposed to do?" I asked and flopped on the bed.

Matthews was a good cop and didn't deserve to get caught up in the middle of this mess. "I know I can't live in ifs; but if I would have been there, he'd still be alive; I just know it! Now what am I supposed to do?" I asked my angel, again.

His face stayed ever emotionless, but his eyes began to shimmer with a blue light. I got up and walked toward him. As I neared him, I could see that the light was coming from within him. He bowed down and met me face-to-face. I looked into his beautiful face and watched the blue light swirl in his eyes. It rolled over itself like ocean waves in a hurricane—spinning and churning until coming to an abrupt stop.

A picture began to form, the outlines blurry. My memories recognized the vision first; it was a church altar, and the priest was at the Mass. Holding the host up and blessing it, I noticed the priest was Father Pete. I hadn't talked to him in weeks and hadn't seen him since the last time I was in New Orleans for confession.

"That's it!" I yelled and flung my arms around, trying to hug my angel. I stumbled through him and remembered no angel hugs. Gathering myself, I smiled wide. Without speaking, my angel had shown me exactly what I needed to do! For the first time in days, hope grew like a mighty oak.

Rushing to my backpack, I grabbed the laptop and fired it up. Clicking around, I found the cyber calling I'd used with Father Pete over the years. Saying a quick prayer, I waited for the computer to fire up. The internet connection of the tiny motel was slow. I waited for the app to load, which was taking much longer than normal. I wiggled in my chair. I put down the computer and paced the room as it dialed in slowly!

"Lavive!" Father Pete exclaimed. "It's so good to see you."

"Oh, Father, it's great to see you; I am so glad I got you on the call!"

"I was about to leave the office and thought I would finish up a few things. And within minutes, you called. It was God's timing for sure!"

We both smiled and made small talk for a few minutes.

"Hold on a moment." Father got up from his chair, and I could hear the door click shut through the computer speakers. "So why did you really call?" His voice intent and quiet.

He knew me too well. "I believe I have a powerful drug demon that is attached to a young woman; and it's strong—the strongest I have seen. It's even influenced someone that wasn't a drug user! I'm lost. I need to help these people, and I have doubts, Father."

"I understand. Your role is so special, and there will be trials along your path; this is just another one. Remember, you are the daughter of a King, and all, no matter their status, must bow before God. Don't get your faith mixed up in your thoughts; keep it in your heart, and you can't ever go wrong. You were made for this; do not doubt yourself."

I took a deep breath; I knew what Father said was true, but I had needed to hear it. "Thank you so much, Father Pete."

"You are very welcome," he paused. "You look tired."

"I am, Father, I am." I rubbed my eyes.

"Take care of yourself, Lavive. No matter the situation, make sure your spiritual and physical self are ready. It sounds like this is a higher-level demon, and you will need all the strength you have to banish it. This situation does sound concerning."

"What do you know about angels and their color?"

"What do you mean?"

"I saw a guardian angel that was pink and

turned maroon; later that night, the girl who belonged with that angel was killed."

"Oh." Father Pete paused. "This may be a new charism you've been given. Prophetic vision will allow you to not only see what others can't, but you can see the near future. That particular charism is not well known; please keep a log on the new details you see with the angels and demons. We will need to see where this leads. Have you seen a black angel?"

"No."

"Good!" Father Pete sounded oddly relieved.

"Why? What's a black angel?" I asked and knew deep inside I didn't ever want to see one.

"It's not of concern right now. I want you to pray. In the meantime, I will also pray and hold a Mass for Rosa today, 4:00 your time."

"Thank you so much!" I felt relief wash over me. Knowing I had Father Pete in my corner calmed my spirit a bit.

"There are things you need to do in order to be ready for this battle. Go to confession, pray and meditate, rest. Clean your side of the street. The demon will use all tactics to attack you; you need to be ready when you go head to head with the Evil One."

"I will, Father." I squared my shoulders. "I will be ready."

TWELVE

I meditated in prayer for what seemed like only minutes; but when I checked the time, hours had passed. It was almost noon. I felt rested and light, like I had slept for ten hours and had a great massage. There was a renewed sense of purpose after the talk with Father Pete. He'd been my confidant and teacher for many years, and I was truly grateful for his instruction and patience.

I dressed in black pants and a black shirt, pulling up my white dreadlocks into a braided bun perched on top of my head, giving me at least three inches of height. Donning my cross-body bag filled with a Bible, holy water, oils, a crucifix, and my prize possession, a relic from the famous Padre Pio.

I had "borrowed" the first class relic from a small church in St. Louis a few years back. I'd return it someday, just not today.

"Lavive?" Tanner's voice echoed through the hollow door; a knock followed. "Lavive, it's Tanner; open up."

Opening the door, there was Tanner, his eyes sunken with dark circles, his hair not in its usual perfect style, but messy and disheveled. "You look like Hell," I noted and opened the door.

"Thanks." Tanner ran a hand through his hair, "I'm just tired. You look fresh as a daisy," he said with a sharp tone in his voice. "Here, I brought food." He threw a bag at me from a local fast food restaurant.

"Thanks, I was talking with a friend." I sat on the bed and unpacked a burger and fries.

"You have friends?" He grumbled as he collapsed in the chair.

"Oh, you are such a funny agent. Yes, I have friends." Fully aware Father Pete was probably my only friend. "A Mass is being held in New Orleans for Rosa, which should really stir the pot around here." I took a huge bite of burger.

Tanner sighed. "Do you think a Mass held hundreds of miles away is going to do anything for this shit storm we are in right now?"

"Wow! That's some attitude you have this afternoon. Yes, the Mass, even though being done states away, will disturb the demon and hopefully draw out Rosa."

"I'm just tired and hungry, Lavive." Bending over, he reached for the bag and pulled out a burger. "I'm sure this will help." He unwrapped the burger and took a giant bite. "Much better," he mumbled.

I nodded and kept eating. I certainly didn't want to get into a psychological debate with a cranky FBI agent. Maybe after he ate.

"Have the cops gotten any leads on Rosa?" I asked between bites.

"No, they're still looking for her and chasing down all other leads. You would be amazed at the number of people that hated Matthews; apparently, he had a reputation around here of being a hard-ass."

I thought of Matthews. Hard-ass or not, I was sure he had family and friends that cared for him. Because I couldn't stop Rosa, he was dead. Near the window, I saw my angel floating in the corner of the room. Beautifully silent. Sometimes I wished I didn't have the human emotions and was more like the angel—calm, stoic, unwavering. Maybe that would make me a better hunter. Pushing down the thoughts of Matthews, I kept eating. I'd deal with those emotions later; there was no time for weakness.

We finished the meals in silence. I looked at my

watch. "Three hours," I whispered.

"Till what?" Tanner asked.

"Father Pete will start the Mass in three hours."

"What is this supposed to do for us here?" He asked while wiping his mouth.

"The Mass will be held for Rosa; it's the best way to get Rosa's intercession and call all the power of the Holy Spirit down to aid in the salvation of her immortal soul."

"You make it sound so dire!"

"It is!" I stressed. "You have to get on board with this, Tanner, and you need to find some mustard seed of faith. This is life and death; we are fighting a war. I do this every day. I know it's hard for you to understand; but believe that I believe, and that will at least be a start."

Tanner dropped his head. "I do believe you," he whispered. "I just don't know if I believe in all this other mumbo-jumbo stuff."

"It's a start." I tilted my head to look him in his hazelnut eyes. "I know you have it in you." We regarded each other for a long moment. He stood up from the chair and came to sit next to me on the bed. I felt my face flush, as he positioned himself right next to me.

"What is it about you?" he asked as he tucked a loose dreadlock behind my ear. "I have never met someone so convicted; you intrigue me, Lavive." His eyes traveled to my lips, and his head tilted.

Without thought or reverence, I leaned in and kissed him.

His lips were surprisingly soft and gentle, too gentle for me. I grabbed the back of his head and deepened our kiss. A low moan came from him, as he wrapped his arms around me. He leaned us back on the bed; at that moment, there were no big bad demons to chase. There wasn't death or fear; there was only light and warmth and the two of us.

I felt my angel near; I could always feel its presence. I opened my eyes slightly and saw beautiful white wings spread out around the two of us. Pulling back, Tanner kissed my neck, and I looked over to my angel. He'd wrapped us in his iridescent wings. It was the most beautiful thing I'd ever seen. The light of Heaven radiated from each feather, and the utter loveliness brought tears to my eyes.

"What's wrong?" Tanner asked and wiped a tear from my cheek.

"Nothing," I said, smiling and letting out a little chuckle. "Absolutely nothing!" I took his face in my hands and kissed him as I had never kissed a man before. I let myself go — really let go.

We laid in angelic bliss, loving and letting love swirl around us like a soft wind in the springtime. The smell of roses permeated the room; I knew instantly that the Holy Mother was near. My heart soared, and joy leaped inside me.

A knock at the door shook our little bubble; Tanner gazed into my eyes, smiled, and kissed my forehead before turning to open the door. My head spun and heart pounded, as I watched him move; somehow, he was even more handsome than he was before the kiss.

Tanner looked outside through the peephole. "Are you expecting someone?" he asked.

"No, why?"

Tanner put his hand on his holstered gun; I jumped up and was at his side as he opened the door.

"Hello." A fresh faced, beautiful, female officer stood at the door. Holding up a badge, she continued, "I am Officer Julie Masters. Agent O'Connely?" She stretched out her arm, a strand of curly red hair fell from the loose bun that held the rest of the red curls at the base of her neck. She was too pretty; I felt a very unfamiliar pang of jealousy settle uncomfortably in my belly.

"Yes." Tanner shook the too pretty officer's hand. "How can I help you?" he asked as he opened the door wider.

"I have been assigned to the Matthews case." She tucked the red strand of hair behind her ear. "I know you have had some conversations with him over the past few days and wanted to pick your brain. His notes said you might be here. It's not every day we get a real FBI profiler in this area of Phoenix."

"Oh well, thank you, Officer. I would be more than willing to discuss the case. Can you give me a few minutes?" Tanner glanced over his shoulder at me.

"Sure, yes, of course," she stammered and backed out of the room.

Tanner shut the door behind her and put his arms around me. I melted into him, instantly feeling better just being in his arms. *What is going on with me?* I thought. I held onto him all the while my mind spun like a top. I couldn't not be attracted to him, and I couldn't not be around him. But I knew that this relationship was dangerous.

"I'm going to go talk to the officer; I will be right back." Tanner kissed me before turning and walking out the door. It clicked shut, and a jolt of energy flooded the room like a tsunami storm surge. I was instantly drowning in reality, and it was suffocating. I fell to my knees, gasping for breath. My fingers dug into the dated shag carpet, as I tried desperately to ground myself. My head hung, and lungs burned, as if breathing fire. I prayed, "Our Father, who art in Heaven, Hallowed be thy name…"

The smell of sulfur permeated the room. I raised my head quickly and searched for the source. "No," I whispered, pulling myself off the ground and hurried out of the motel room. I searched around the area outside of the motel, and there was no sign of Tanner or Officer Julie Masters, if that was even her real name. "Shit!" I cursed and ran across to the diner. *It had only been minutes. Where are they?* I thought.

Coming back to the motel parking lot, I noticed Tanner's black Buick still parked in front of my room; there wasn't another car in the lot. As I got closer to the Buick, something odd stuck out—something red, blood red. I went over to the windshield and saw it—a rose. My blood turned to ice as the hair on the back of my neck raised up. This wasn't just a coincidence; Tanner had been taken.

"Dammit!" I grabbed the red rose and tore it apart; petals fell across the blacktop, like I'd been throwing them on a casket as it was lowered into a grave. That cop, or a fake cop, or possessed cop—whatever the pretty, young thing was—worked for Rosa and the drug demon. I wasn't sure how or why, but I was sure that Tanner was in trouble. And he probably didn't even know yet. His lack of conviction would be his downfall if I couldn't get to him before Rosa did. If she was as powerful as I believed, there was no limit to her influence on him. No matter how big and strong he thought he was? This demon was cunning and would do anything to get its way. Guilt rushed over me. Each person I saw taken, each person I had gotten close to would die or worse. I thought of Emily, Kevin, Matthews, and now Tanner—doubt crept in.

"How am I supposed to save Tanner, save Rosa, fight the higher-level demon, and win?" I screamed at my angel.

He floated peacefully around me, which was extremely aggravating. "If I could just get Tanner, that would be something, although I don't have a clue where they took him! Help me!" I couldn't fight the anger and fear that gripped me like a vice.

I sat on the curb, a glint of red on the edge of my shoe caught my eye. A rose petal had stuck to the bottom of my shoe; I peeled it out of the treads of my boots and rubbed the petal between my pointer finger and thumb, releasing the sweet smell of the rose. I prayed a Hail Mary and let the aroma of the rose fill my senses.

My angel bent toward me and met my eyes; I stared into his blue pools. He showed me Rosa, looking into her eyes that were dark pools, and reflected back was my own image. I watched the vision of me change, as light began to appear. Slowly, a white house came into the vision. It was three stories tall and old, but still stunning. The windows and doorways were arched, and I noticed a stained glass window but couldn't make out the design. I didn't recognize the house, but there was only one reason I'd been shown it; I needed to go there. That was where I'd find answers and maybe Tanner, too. But how was I going to find this house in a city as big as Phoenix?

"Where?" I asked my angel.

The vision backed up, higher and higher, showing the streets of the area and the surrounding buildings; then it went even higher. Finally, I noticed in the lower corner of the vision the bus depot, diner, and motel.

Taking a mental picture, I thanked my angel for letting me see the location of the house. I got up and went back to my room. It was the same as it was before, but I was different. Internally, there was hope, light, and love. Even with looking into the darkness, I brought back light with me. I wasn't an angel, but I was lucky to have such a great one by my side.

I drew a rudimentary map of what I had seen in the vision on a scrap of paper from my bag.

"All right!" I said with conviction, gathering my bag of tools. "Time to find that house and get Tanner." I nodded to my angel and headed out the door, into the unknown. But I wasn't scared, not even concerned. *Walk by faith*, I thought.

The desert air was dry, and the sun hung low, turning the sky hues of orange and pinks. *A beautiful night for some demon ass-kicking*, I thought and kept moving down the street. I knew the house in my vision must be close. There weren't that many parts of Phoenix that were old and worn down, plus my past had proven that a demon doesn't run too far from its comfort zone. Rosa would be near. I followed the map I had drawn based on the vision.

I rounded the corner and glanced back at the darkened Waffle House. I thought of Matthews and the others that had died at the hands of this drug demon. I wanted nothing more than to cast it back to Hell.

I looked down the street, trying to find the large white house I'd seen in my vision. A few dilapidated, small houses dotted the street. A broken chain fence surrounded one. Two homeless men stood on a corner the next block up. It was quiet. Then suddenly, I heard yelling and a crash. The two homeless guys were fighting, and one had knocked over the other's grocery cart full of his belongings. I couldn't hear exactly what they were saying; but by the tone and shoving, it was escalating quickly. Another yell, to my left, caught my attention. A woman was screaming at her kids. To my right, I saw a man that was obviously not stable, fighting with invisible people. *What in the hell?* I thought

Then it hit me. I looked at my watch—it had begun.

THIRTEEN

It was 4:00 pm — the dedication Mass for Rosa had started in New Orleans. Father Pete was conducting the Mass for her freedom from her oppression. I looked around and saw the chaos unfolding on the streets. As I watched the people fight around me, I realized just how strong the drug demon was, and it was influencing not only Rosa but the entire area. I knew no matter how far away a Mass was performed, it would affect the person the Mass is dedicated to. Even so, I was surprised to see it to affecting the entire neighborhood. The demon's hold on the area was stronger than I had thought. A twinge of hesitation settled in my chest. I snuffed it out with a quick St.

Michael prayer.

Following the sound of yelling and fighting, I rounded the corner and spotted a group of people tussling over a metal grocery cart, outside a large house. The massive house stood out on the street of tiny one-story bungalows. The peeling white stucco building was foreboding, and a darkness fell over the house. The arched windows on the first floor were boarded up, although the second-floor glass ones were intact. The roof was old with clay tiles, many missing and littering the grounds around the house. I noticed the ornate stained glass window on the second floor, a picture of a large cactus set against a background of mountains with a sunrise and colorful sky and a horned skull in the lower left corner. It was beautiful, a stark contrast to the darkness of the house. My heart skipped a beat; this was the house from the vision.

Quickening my pace, I pushed past the angry people and stood at the bottom stair in front of the house. My stomach turned, and sweat trickled down my back. Rosa was inside; I could feel it. I hope Tanner was too. A few men were arguing in front of the massive wooden door. The door was framed on each side by two unmaintained, large shrubs that reached up to the second floor.

I quietly slipped past the men by squeezing behind one of the shrub trees. I was still in shock on how the Mass was affecting the people around the house, keeping everyone distracted with aggravation.

Once inside, I could see that it was just as run down as the outside. I stood in the once opulent foyer and looked around, trying to feel where to go next. The rooms were separated by grand archways, each at least ten feet tall. To the right was a front parlor room, remnants of old curtains and a tattered dusty rug were left. A torn-up couch sat awkwardly in the center of the room. To the left was a dining room where a large chandelier, missing many crystals, hung haphazardly, ready to fall at any moment. I felt evil everywhere. My hand went instinctively to the blue-beaded rosary that I was wearing around my neck. I prayed an Our Father and a Hail Mary. My hands itched, and I concentrated on the power of prayer until a loud thud from the second floor distracted me.

I shot off and took the stairs two at a time. Following the noise, I took a right at the top of the stairs, where there was a long hallway with four doors. To the left was another short hallway with two doors. Each hallway had a large stained-glass window; they were much bigger than I'd realized when standing on the street.

My breath quickened. I prayed and glanced back and forth, right and left, looking for Rosa. Lifting my hands, one toward each side, I closed my eyes and prayed. My palms tingled, as the power of the prayer emanated from my body. A white ball of energy burst out of my right palm and quickly flew down the long hall, disappearing as it crashed into the last door.

I took off toward the last door on the right. Grabbing the knob, it twisted on its own. I stood there for a moment; my eyes focused on the doorknob. Was someone opening the door for me? I pushed the door, but it didn't give. Throwing myself against the door, I pushed with all my might. It began to budge. I could hear soft moaning coming from the other side.

"Tanner?" I pushed harder. "I'm here. Are you in there?" Another moan. "I'm coming!" I threw myself against the door, and it moved about a foot, just enough for me to slide into the room. "Tanner?" I called out as I squeezed through the door.

Inside, I saw Tanner, tied up behind the door, his hands taped together, and his mouth covered. Our eyes met.

"I'm here." I bent down and peeled off the tape from his mouth.

"Lavive, you have to get out of here. Call the cops. Get back up. You have no idea what—" He trailed off, as his head wobbled. I searched the room, checking every corner. I didn't see anyone. I closed the door behind me and locked it.

"It's going to be okay," I said and took out a

pocketknife from my cross-body bag. I cut his hands loose and placed him on his back. I checked him over for wounds and couldn't see any blood. His left eye was swollen and bruised. His pupils were bloodshot and fully dilated.

He moaned again and garbled some incoherent words. I looked around the old room for some clue as to what was wrong with him. There was a chair, an old desk, and a door that led to a small bathroom. I jumped up, still on guard for Rosa or any of her minions, and ran to the bathroom, hoping the water in the old house still worked. It did! I wet a piece of gauze that I had in my bag and turned to attend to Tanner.

Something caught my eye, and I stopped. I recognized the glint of silver; there was a spoon behind the door. I closed the door and saw the drug set up on the back of the white toilet—a spoon, lighter, syringe, and rubber band that would have been used for a tourniquet.

Immediately, I thought of Matthews! Tanner had been drugged, too! By the way he was acting, he was on the verge of an overdose. My heart quickened. I didn't have any methadone on me, of course, and my holy water wasn't going to do much good against whatever concoction some demon had given him.

"Shit!" I grabbed the spoon and tucked it in a pocket of my bag. Running back to Tanner, he was in and out of consciousness. "Tanner, stay with me." He opened his eyes a bit. "We have to get out of here; you have to help me. Where is your phone?" He wobbled his head. *Dammit!* I thought.

Looking around the room, I saw my angel hovering near the chair. I went to him and got down on my hands and knees. I searched around the floor when my hand grazed a small square, and my heart leapt into my throat.

I pulled the square out. But it wasn't a phone like I expected. It was a small wooden box. It looked as if it was hand carved with care and possibly an antique. Not knowing its significance, I tucked the box in my bag and kept searching for the phone.

I looked up to my angel. "Please, help me!" I begged. I saw his face move the slightest bit, and his brows scrunched as a human would show concern. Here was my angel doing something different again—showing human emotion—but I couldn't think of the shock of it right now. I had to find a phone to save Tanner.

"Lavive," Tanner moaned.

"Shit!" I jumped up and ran to his side. "Come on, Tanner, you're going to have to help me a little."

"I believe you," he whispered.

Tears stung my eyes as I watched Tanner. In his drugged state, he wasn't the strong FBI agent I'd come to admire; there was an innocence and vulnerability.

I noticed old, thick curtains on the windows. Then an angel appeared; but not any angel, it was Tanner's guardian angel. I watched his angel float near the window with its wings outstretched, reaching across the entire room. It opened its hands, and thin rays of light flowed from its palms toward Tanner. The rays of light entered his chest. Tanner's angel was trying to help him. Its face was a beautiful translucent blue, but the tips of his wings were turning pink, almost maroon. My breath caught in my throat.

I moved quickly to the window. Grabbing a curtain, I ripped it off the wall and laid it next to Tanner. "Come on, roll a little." I pulled him toward me and tucked the fabric of the curtain under him. I got his legs on the curtain and bunched it up around his shoulders - making two handles. "We can do this!" I announced with all the conviction I had and pulled with all my might.

The initial movement was hard, but once the momentum started, I was able to pull Tanner along the wooden floor of the room, out into the hallway. Inch by inch, foot by foot, we moved. My arms burned, and I was quickly losing feeling in my fingers; but I wasn't stopping. As we neared the stairs, it dawned on me. How was I going to get this massive man down the stairs—a log roll?

The overwhelming smell of sulfur froze me mid-pull. "Shit," I whispered and bent to Tanner. "Don't move."

"You found him, señorita! ¡Muy bien!" Rosa strolled up the stairs, wearing a red flowing dress; her hair pulled up with a rose tucked behind her ear. She looked as if she had stepped out of a movie. Her movements were fluid, and the dress billowed with each step she took. The strapless neckline plunged into a deep V at her chest, showing off her hourglass figure. I watched her glide up the stairs with ease. She was the epitome of beauty; the kind men wrote songs about.

"Do you think I will let you take him?" Her head tilted to one side, and a slight smile settled on her glossy red lips.

"I am taking him, and I am banishing you, demon!"

Rosa laughed, a light-hearted chuckle at first, but it gradually grew to a deep growl that shook the old house. Her face grimaced, and the beauty it held disappeared. My palms itched, as I pressed them together in prayer. I recited prayers of deliverance in the tongue of the angels while slowly rubbing my palms together. I could feel the power grow, as I began another prayer.

"No, no, no, Deliverer." Rosa wagged her finger. "Not today, señorita." Rosa seemingly flew up the last ten steps and landed directly in front of me.

Jumping back, I raised my hands in defense; the white light burned bright from my palms. Rosa ducked, her arm raised, shielding her eyes.

"You know there is no way to win; it's not possible," I said.

"It may not be possible to defeat Him; but you, señorita, are just a tiny, little human girl." Rosa looked me in the eye; her smile had become a gritted snarl.

I stared at her black eyes. The Rosa who was, was no longer; I was looking into the eyes of a fully possessed Rosa.

Suddenly, she bent into a crouching position and kicked one leg out in a sweeping motion. Rosa swept my legs out from underneath me. I flipped backward, landing hard on the wooden floor. I moaned and turned to the side. The light in my palms was gone. It was hard enough to get the power of prayer when I concentrated; but with Rosa's Karate-Kid-sweep-the-leg move, there was no way I could keep it.

"Ouch! That hurt!" I yelled and rolled onto my knees. "I'm going to love sending you back to Hell."

Rosa was behind me, standing over Tanner. He was still wrapped in the old curtain and out cold from the drugs. "Ohhhh, he may not make it. Do you see? His breathing is shallow, and I can feel he's close to the other side." Rosa tilted her head.

"Whatever will you do? Save the man or fight me?"

I studied Tanner and knew she was right. If I didn't get him to a hospital soon, he wasn't going to live. I looked back up to Rosa; her smug smile lit a fire in me. I saw his angel behind her and knew what to do. I prayed the St. Michael prayer, as my hands began to burn with light. Raising my hands as I yelled, "Amen," two arcs of light flew from my palms and hit Rosa square in the chest. The thunder of the light sizzled in the air.

Rosa flew down the hall and crashed through a stained glass window. I fell to my knees and breathed heavily. I had never produced a lightning bolt before. I didn't even know it was possible, but the flying demon told me it was now possible. I crawled to the side of the hallway and pulled myself to standing. I ran down the hall and peered out the window.

Examining the ground, I expected to find a mangled Rosa, but there was nothing but glass. I let out an audible sigh. She was gone. She survived the fall. She'd be back, but for now, I needed to take care of Tanner.

He was still passed out. I figured it was better this way; I was going to have to pull him down the stairs, and I was sure it was not going to be fun for him. I grabbed the curtain and pulled. Each step, each thud, each groan, we moved closer to the front door. I opened the door, and all the people who had been out front fighting were gone. I was hoping someone could help me, but I guessed I was on my own. Seeing the grocery cart gave me an idea.

Kicking the railing off the side of the porch, I put Tanner on the edge. Pulling the cart up to the house, I aligned it near Tanner. I pushed him off the porch and prayed he landed in the cart. Success!

I rolled down the street, Tanner squished into the wire grocery cart like some oversized baby. I was sure we looked ridiculous, but it was this or dragging him. I preferred the oversized baby. I stopped at the first intersection and tried to wave for cars to stop. I needed someone to call an ambulance. I couldn't push him all the way to the hospital in this grocery cart.

The first few cars sped past me, and then finally, someone pulled over. I asked them to call an ambulance.

"You're going to be okay," I reassured Tanner as we waited for the ambulance.

"Lavive," he whispered. "I believe you. She is evil. Be careful."

FOURTEEN

The ambulance came and took Tanner to the hospital. I didn't go; I needed to look for Rosa or at least get some sense of where she went. I gave the syringe, spoon, and address of the house to the officer who came and took my statement. I didn't catch his name; I was too distracted.

The demon had gone too far with the attack on Tanner. I knew it was just trying to hurt me, but it underestimated my heart. I wasn't going to cry and be a pitiful sad sack; it just pissed me off!

Back in my motel room, I changed clothes and washed my face; there was no time for rest. Gathering my things, including a new can of mace and refilling my holy water, I went back out to look for Rosa. It was getting dark, and the night had a chill to it. I wrapped my leather jacket tight around me. I patrolled a few blocks surrounding the motel and diner but didn't feel anything out of the ordinary. I knew the feeling of evil when it was near. It was similar to feeling scared and angry at the same time. The hairs on my arms would stand on end, but I could throat punch someone, too. It was a weird mix of emotions—that was the tell-tale sign that a damned one is near.

Rounding a corner for the third time, I saw a couple of men huddled together about a block away. Walking toward them, I recognized the shorter one. I had seen him in the diner the night Kevin died. I quickened my step.

"Hey!" I called.

One of the men glanced at me. The tall one grinned, not a nice grin, the kind of smile that made my skin crawl. The shorter one with brown hair didn't look up; he was busy fiddling on his phone.

"Hey, wait a second!" I said as I trotted up to the men; my hand, firmly placed in my bag, tightened around my second can of mace. *I need a gun*, I thought.

"What can I do for you, pretty lady?" The tall one took a few steps toward me and tilted his head. I wanted to punch that guy but worked on keeping my composure.

"Hi," I said to the shorter guy, completely bypassing the tall one.

His huff let me know he wasn't thrilled. "Hey, Mitchell, this little hot piece is talking to you. Put that stupid phone down," the tall guy barked.

"I saw you the other night in the diner with Kevin," I said, as his head snapped up.

"Kevin?" he said and locked eyes with me for the first time. I could see the swirl of black smoke encircle the whites of his eyes. He wasn't damned but certainly marked. "Where is Kevin?" he asked, his voice almost childlike.

"I'm sorry, but Kevin died."

He didn't blink but stared as if processing the words I just said.

"Oh," he whispered and looked back to his phone.

I looked at the phone, which was a newer model. How could these two transients afford a phone like the one Tanner had?

"Hey, where did you get that phone?" I asked and took a step toward Mitchell.

"It's mine." He tucked it in his pocket. "Master gave it to me."

I perked up. "Do you know where Kevin went the other night?" I said, trying to pry useful info from these two. "Do you know Rosa?"

He looked up, the dark swirls in his eyes beginning to spin faster. I watched the black swirls thicken.

"Who are you?" he asked as he took a few steps toward me.

My palms began to burn, and I knew I was dealing with the demon that was trying to take over this man, not the man anymore. Mitchell was gone for now. I was face-to-face with yet another one. It seemed Rosa's drug demon had a large army of minor demons working with it. Father Pete said this might be the case; I was sure now it certainly was!

I gave a quick side-eye look to the big guy, who also took a step toward me. He wasn't damned, but a creeper for sure. My right hand tightened around my mace.

"Hey, I'm a friend. I was a friend of Kevin's and Emily's. Did you know Emily?" I asked quickly.

"We know everyone around here, and you are not from here." Mitchell stepped closer.

"Don't," I warned as I prayed the St. Michael prayer, and my palms began to glow. I kept the left fisted and the right in my purse; people tended to freak out about glowing hands. I didn't use my powers in front of people if I didn't have to.

The tall guy loomed over me, and my breath caught in my throat. The different scenarios and outcomes swam in my mind. I was going to have to act and act fast to get out of this situation unharmed. I started to pull out the mace.

"I think we should get to know this girl a little better," the tall one said and rubbed the front of his dirty jeans.

"No, this girl is all mine," Mitchell said as his eyes glazed over like black marbles.

Dammit, I thought and pulled out my mace.

"Stay back!" I held the mace in front of me and pointed it back and forth from the tall one to Mitchell.

"You can't get us both," the tall one said and then lurched toward me.

I sprayed. He tackled me to the ground; the yells and cursing told me the mace had made contact. I kicked and crawled out from under him while he was busy tending to his burning eyes. I pushed off the sidewalk and stood, moving my dreadlocks from my face. I extended my hands toward Mitchell who hadn't moved.

"Tell me where she is!" I demanded.

"We will not help you, Deliverer!" he growled.

"Fine," I said and jumped forward, tackling him to the sidewalk next to the tall guy who was still screaming in pain.

Mitchell thrashed, but the power flowing from my hands kept him at bay. I prayed in tongues and focused on the deliverance of the man. I knew banishing this lower-level demon wasn't going to give me Rosa, but the best thing I could do was cast its demon ass back to Hell. My hands glowed bright, and I felt the Holy Spirit flow through me.

The screeching of tires caught my attention. I looked down the street to see a white truck speeding our way. I continued to pray as the truck approached quickly. I couldn't let go, or the demon wouldn't be cast out. I held onto Mitchell's face and prayed.

The truck came to a halt, and I heard the driver yell as she opened the door, "Get in; she wants us."

I concentrated on my hands and the Spirit flowing through me; I didn't see the boot until it was too late. As it made contact with my chest, I flew backwards and hit the sidewalk hard. Pain shot through my back, as I tried to catch my breath.

"What is wrong with you? You showed yourself to the Deliverer!" the female who stood over me yelled at the men.

Somewhere, I had heard that voice before, but it wasn't Rosa. I clutched my chest, able to get to my side. I watched Mitchell and the driver get in the front of the truck and the taller man crawl in the back, still rubbing his eyes. Mustering all I had left, I stood and took a few steps closer, able to see inside the truck. I caught a glimpse of red hair.

"Where is she?" I demanded breathlessly. Pretty ballsy of me, considering there were three of them and one of me.

As I walked a few steps closer, my mouth gaped

open.

"Don't worry, little Deliverer. She will come to you soon." Officer Julie Masters, who had taken Tanner earlier, smirked and the truck sped off.

"That bitch!" I said as they drove out of sight. Falling to my knees I held my chest, not only the impact of her boot but the emotional pain rocked through me. I had failed again. It hurt to breathe. The day's events swam through my mind: finding Tanner drugged and almost dying, fighting Rosa, and now this mess in the streets of Phoenix. I raised my head to the stars. "Why?" My head dropped, as I knew there wouldn't be an answer.

I pushed off the ground and stood on shaky legs. No matter the pain, I had to find that cop and the other two henchmen. The demon attached to Rosa must be a very powerful demon to have all these lower demons doing its bidding. I was sick of this demon frat party and was going to do everything in my power to end it all.

I tried to take a deep breath and winced. I held my chest and walked toward the streetlamp, leaning on it. The night's events raced through my head. If Officer Masters was to be trusted, she had promised Rosa would find me when ready. In that moment, I was in no condition to fight Rosa — shit, I couldn't even face a minor demon right now. I decided to head back to my motel and prepare for the ultimate battle.

When I returned to my room, I wrapped my chest in a tight bandage, took a few pain pills, and hailed a taxi.

"Where to?" the driver asked as I carefully climbed in the back.

I relaxed against the black, leather seat. "The main office of the Catholic Diocese of Phoenix."

FIFTEEN

I knew the Catholic Diocese of Phoenix wouldn't be open, considering it was midnight, but I'd wait. The taxi pulled down an empty street and stopped in front of a curved brick sign with large letters that read, "Roman Catholic Church of Phoenix." I looked toward the sign again, and my angel floated near the end of the semi-circle. I wasn't sure where he had been when I was fighting the short, possessed guy and Officer Masters pulled up, but I was glad to see him now.

I paid the driver with the last of my money and headed toward the entrance of the compound. To the right was a small grotto; I heard the water trickling. The large, square building was two stories tall surrounded by a brick and black iron fence. The sidewalk pillar lights lit the path to the gate entrance. The gate was about nine-feet tall, made of black metal. I wrapped my hands around the cold bars and pulled, but they didn't budge. I figured as much. I knew the priests would be up at sunrise to open, so I had a few hours to wait and decided to walk the front grounds.

The large trees that surrounded the building branched in all directions and created a canopy of green leaves, like a cover that blotted out the stars. I headed into the middle of the trees, following the sidewalks. I heard the water before I saw the fountain.

The large, round fountain was made of brick and stone; the water fluttered out of the six spouts at the top ring and flowed down into a larger second ring. I sat on the ledge and listened to the water. Closing my eyes, I focused on the peaceful lapping. Moving down to the cobblestone ground, I leaned against one of the brick pillars. Exhaling, I relaxed my body and my mind. It had been a hard day. My chest ached, and my mind whirled with thoughts of Rosa, Tanner, Officer Masters, Mitchell, and all the possible henchmen whom I'd have to address. I was already exhausted.

A warm breeze got my attention, and I opened my eyes; my angel floated near me. I looked up as he knelt. His face shown a beautiful, peaceful blue.

"I'm tired," I said as a tear escaped. He lifted his hand and caressed my cheek. His touch was as soft as silk. With a large swish of air, his wings expanded outwards. As they opened wide, I watched the light dance off the iridescent feathers. They shone as if covered by millions of tiny diamonds. My mouth fell open, at the wonder of it all. He hardly ever showed his full span of wings to me — just one other time in the past five years. I checked to make sure they were all white.

The protection they provided was even better than their beauty. His wings flexed, and then curved to wrap around me. Closing my eyes, I let the feeling of love radiate through me. He was, after all, the embodiment of God's love. Being wrapped in his wings was as if God was holding me Himself.

I left myself relax. I was safe and protected. I could let go, and I did. One thing I had learned over the past years was that when I had a chance to really relax, I'd better do it. Demon hunting was really freaking stressful!

The time melted away, as he stayed with me; I hadn't noticed I fell asleep.

"Miss?" I felt a tap on my shoulder and jerked up.

"What!" I yelled, scaring the priest that stood in front of me.

"Are you okay? You were sleeping by the

fountain."

"Oh, yes, thank you." My words stumbled out of my mouth as I stood. My body was stiff from sleeping on stone.

The priest reached out his hand; I took it to steady myself.

"Thank you." I stretched as much as the pain would allow.

"I am Father Kauna; can I help you with something?" His brown eyes drew together as he looked intently at me. I couldn't imagine what a train wreck I must have looked like, sleeping on the ground outside a church in the middle of the night. Pretty symbolic of my life.

"Yes, you can, Father. I need confession. Would you or any other priest have time this morning?" I knew that one of the honors of being a priest was hearing confession, to be that intercessor between the people and God; he'd always say yes when asked.

"Of course." Father Kauna motioned toward the gate entrance. "Let us go to the chapel." I noticed his accent.

Picking up my bag, I followed the priest, noticing his height for the first time. He must have been at least six foot five; his cassock covered a thin frame, reminding me of a runner's body type.

"How long have you been in Phoenix, Father?" I asked.

"I have been here two years; I transferred from Kenya."

"Oh wow! What a change."

He laughed. "Yes, it was an adjustment, but I have come to love the people of Phoenix."

We stopped in front of the chapel. Father Kauna unlocked the door with the giant ring of keys he kept on his hip. The doors opened; and as I stepped inside the building, I felt the presence of God. I closed my eyes, taking in the internal divine glow of the church.

"This way." Father motioned me to the side of the chapel, where the confessionals were built into the walls of the church. Wood stretched from the floors to the pews and up to the rafters. Stained glass depictions of holy events covered each window, letting in the morning sun in streaks of reds, blues, and gold. "Please." He motioned toward the small, wooden door.

I knelt in the confessional, facing the screen. I could make out the silhouette of Father Kauna on the other side. I hadn't been to confession without Father Pete in years. Suddenly apprehensive, I wasn't sure how Father Kauna would react to all the crazy-ass demon-chasing stories. Erring on the side of caution, I decided to keep the gritty details for my confessions with Father Pete and focus on my internal confession of sins.

Making the sign of the cross, we began.

*   *   *

We finished up the confession and left the tiny rooms.

"Thank you, Father," I said and shook his hand.

"Of course," he said and smiled wide. I wondered what he thought of me; but I knew as a priest, he'd leave the confession with God and not carry my sins with him.

"Father, I'm also here to gather my payment for the month."

"Your payment?" His eyebrows arched.

"Yes, if you check your records, you should have an envelope for me. I am hired by the church to investigate the demonic activity around the US."

"OH! Yes, I do know about that; I haven't thought of it for a while. I was told when I arrived to give you an envelope if you ever showed up in Phoenix." He smiled. "You are not what I expected!"

"Ha! Yeah, I get that a lot." I laughed and tucked a white dreadlock behind my ear.

"Let's go to my office, and I can get the envelope from the safe."

We walked through the chapel, outside, and then down the perfectly landscaped path to another white stucco building. The morning sun warmed the air as the large palm trees swayed in a slight breeze. Entering a smaller building, we climbed the stairs to his office. He unlocked the door and welcomed me into the room.

It was filled with books and paper stacks in tall bookcases that lined three of the walls. "You must like reading," I said and ran my fingers across the spines of a row of books.

"Yes, I am an avid reader and love to learn," he said and bent down to the small safe that was stored behind his desk. "Here it is!" he exclaimed and waved a white envelope in the air.

"Great." I walked toward the desk as he locked the safe and stood to meet me.

"Here you are," he passed the envelope to me. "Be safe," Father said as I noticed his guardian angel in the corner of the room, floating near a short stack of books on the ground. It was similar to mine, but each had their own small differences. This one, like most angels of religious life people, had a shining gold cross on its chest. He was beautiful. I looked back to Father and smiled wide.

"I will, Father, I promise." I sat in one of the two leather chairs and pulled my cross-body bag up into my lap. Flipping open the lid, I pulled out the half empty bottle of holy water, blessed oil, blessed salt, and my relic of Padre Pio. I heard a gasp and looked at the priest. He quickly made the sign of the cross and stared at the relic.

"Oh, yes, it is what you think."

His eyes never left the small glass container that

held a small piece of knuckle bone from Padre Pio's right hand. "Would you like to hold it?" I asked.

"I—I couldn't," he stammered. His hand shook as he extended it toward the relic.

"Here," I picked up the glass case and tossed it to him. I thought he might cry, as he reached up and caught the small case. Falling to his knees, he cradled the item like a baby. "I want that back," I said as he looked up at me with tears in his eyes.

Father Kauna smiled and turned it over and over in his hands. He'd moved to the chair next to me, and I watched the grown man grow absolutely giddy!

"You are a fan of Padre Pio?" I asked and pulled out a few more items in my bag.

"Yes," he whispered. I could hear him quietly praying as he held the artifact. "I met him once, years ago, when I was a young boy in the Nyanza Province of Kenya. He was passing through and stopped just to talk to me; I felt so special."

"That's so sweet," I said and glanced over at Father Kauna's angel; I wondered if Padre Pio had this same gift, maybe even back then, when he was just a boy. Padre could see the gold cross a guardian angel wore on its chest. If he did see one, then he knew that child was meant to be a priest. So, it makes sense that he would have stopped to meet Father Kauna. Maybe Padre Pio and I had more in common than I thought.

I pulled out the wooden box that I had found in the house, where Tanner had been drugged and left for dead. I narrowed my eyes and set it on the desk. I didn't know I could hate an inanimate object.

"What is that?" Father Kauna said and jumped from the chair, making the sign of the cross three times and holding the relic out as a shield.

"What? It's a box I found in a building."

"May I see it?" He was already picking it up.

I watched him turn it around in his hands, holding it as carefully as he did the relic. Sitting the box on his desk, Father clutched the relic in his left hand and carefully opened the hinged lid of the box with his right. I peered over his shoulder to see what was inside. I hadn't even had the thought to open it yet. His hand was trembling as he took out the first item; it was a lock of dark hair tied with a red ribbon. He set it aside. The next item was a dried out red rose; I thought of Rosa. He took out a piece of paper next and carefully unfolded it.

Father gasped and folded the paper back up quickly.

"What is it?" I asked.

"What I thought." He placed all the items back into the box carefully and closed the lid. "Where did you find this?"

"At an abandoned house where I was searching for a woman that I believe is possessed."

"She is," he said flatly.

"How are you certain?"

"This isn't just any box; this is a curse. I have seen this in Kenya many years ago. A family had come to me for prayer; they had been plagued with many ailments, and it was escalating quickly. During the blessing of their home, I found a similar grouping of items in a pillow. It was a curse that had been placed on the family from a rival family clan. It is a powerful curse that brings with it the worst of the demonic powers." His brows drew together, and he bit his lower lip. "This particular curse can cause the person whom it was intended for to be vulnerable to the Evil One. How did you come about this box?"

"Like I said, I just found it. I believe the woman whom this is intended for is possessed by a higher-level drug demon, one that has a big hold on the community and possible numerous minor demons working for it."

"I am not surprised to hear this. This curse invokes all the powers of the Evil One and his minions." Father Kauna sat in his desk chair.

"What do I do? How do I undo this?" I asked. I couldn't believe I had been so distracted that I didn't realize it was a curse, although I had been trained in demonology—not in Kenya curses.

"There is much you can do," he paused and riffled through some papers. "Here it is!" He held up two sheets of paper. "This should work for you." He handed me the papers and the Padre Pio relic. "Use them both at the place you found the box; it must be at the same place. This will draw the demon to you, so prepare yourself."

I nodded and took the papers. The title of the article read, "St. Padre Pio Procedure to Destroy Occult or Cursed Objects."

"Thank you, Father," I said and tucked all the items carefully back into my shoulder bag. "Is there anything else I need to know?"

"Be careful." He placed his large hands on top of my head and prayed in his native language. I couldn't understand the words, but I could feel the power.

Father Kauna called me a cab and guided me to the edge of the grounds. His face laced with worry.

"I will be fine, Father. This isn't my first demon banishing." I smiled, trying to lighten the mood.

"Go with God, my child." His hand lightly squeezed my shoulder as the taxi drove up the curved drive.

I got into the taxi and thanked him again through my rolled down window. I wondered if the Padre Pio prayers and destroying of the relic of the family in Kenya worked. He never finished the end of the story.

SIXTEEN

I read the papers as the taxi drove toward my motel. The ritual consisted of prayers, holy water, and fire—I could handle that.

The taxi dropped me off, and I called the hospital from the motel office phone. I wanted to see Tanner, but I had work to do. I had spent more time at the diocese than I thought I would have to, and I needed to get back to hunting Rosa.

"Hey!" Tanner hollered. "How are you? Where have you been? I really hate that you don't have a cell phone."

"Why, so you can stalk me?" I smiled.

"Maybe," he said in a soft voice

My face flushed, and I was glad he couldn't see

me. "Are you feeling better?"

"Yeah, they're getting all the drugs out of my system. I should be out of here soon. I don't know how people like doing drugs; it made me feel so out of control."

"That's exactly why people like it."

"How are you doing?" he asked.

"Fine," I lied.

"What's wrong?"

"It's nothing, just a kick to the ribs."

"Who?"

"It was that Officer Julie Masters fake person that tricked you."

He mumbled something.

"She's also possessed by some other lower-level demon, seems they are working as a large team."

"I can't wait to arrest that bit—"

"Tanner!"

He stopped.

"It's fine. I have this under control. I have a plan. We just need to get you better. Try to let me do my job."

He was silent, and I could imagine him fuming in that hospital bed.

"What happened once you went with Officer Masters? How did all this—" I paused. "Happen?"

"I've been thinking about that all day; I can't really figure it out. I did it. I took the drugs, but it was as if somehow all my convictions disappeared, and all that was left was wanting to do drugs. They were there; Rosa was there, and she told me I would be okay, that I would like it." He cleared his throat. "I just don't know how—"

"Was there a spell or did you smell or drink anything?"

"A spell?" He laughed. "No, it wasn't a spell."

"I only ask because Rosa has been cursed by a very powerful Kenya curse, and I need to address it as soon as possible."

"I thought you were all church, angels, and demons. What's this about curses and spells?"

"I'm trying to teach you something, if you could just listen and not argue, that'd be great," I said sharply.

"Sorry, Lavive, go on," he said.

"I'm a Catholic and have strong beliefs, but I'm not stupid. I know there are many avenues for the Evil One to integrate in our world. One of those is through curses. This form of witchery has been around for thousands of years. I must know and respect all forms of evil that comes from all the corners of the world and keep my own personal relationship with God on the right path. It's all very confusing." I paused and thought of my training with Father Pete. "I believe Rosa has been cursed and with that came the demon that was able to possess her."

"So, she's not responsible?" he asked, and I

imagined his brow crinkling like it did when he thought I was talking crazy.

"I'm not saying that. I'm saying there are other forces in action here. Like you." I fiddled with the old school phone cord. "You took the drug; you made the choice, even if it was blurry. It was still a choice."

"I didn't want to do drugs, certainly not almost die from an overdose."

"Right! That's what I'm saying. I know it's muddy, but we have choice. But sometimes, God allows us to be influenced by the Evil One—"

"Why? That seems ridiculous."

"We will never know all the reasons, but faith allows me to know there IS a reason for all of it. For example, if you were never under the influence, then maybe you wouldn't be so willing to listen and possibly believe."

Tanner sat silent for a minute, and I tried to let him think; but I really needed to start looking for Rosa

"I have to go."

I heard Tanner begin to say something, but I cut him off. "I need to go back to that house and find Rosa; I have to stop this."

"I'm going, too," Tanner said, and I heard sounds of the phone being moved around. "Don't even start a fight, Lavive. I am going."

"No, you need to stay safe, to stay there."

"I'm going. You don't have a gun or any protection; you don't even have a cell phone!" he was yelling. "What am I supposed to do? Let you confront these people who may or may not be possessed by the Devil all alone?"

"Yes, which is exactly what I want you to do," I said trying to reason with him. "I've done this many times before; I know what I'm doing."

"I know you do." I heard him stop moving around and pause for a moment. "I know you can take care of yourself. You're the most competent woman I've ever met. I need my own resolution to this situation, too. She won't influence me again."

"I believe you, Tanner. But I have to do this alone. Pray for me." I hung up the phone and imagined Tanner cussing up a storm on the other end.

I closed my eyes and breathed in deep. My chest still ached a little, but it was tolerable. I opened my eyes; my guardian angel stood behind me with his wings wrapped around me. It should have brought me comfort, and it would have, if the tips of his wings weren't maroon in color.

My stomach knotted; the last and only time I had ever seen an angel turn maroon was Emily's angel the night she died. Was I going to die? I turned quickly and looked at my angel in the face, searching for some insight. His face shown a blue light, but his features didn't make any human expression I could read. He was even more frustrating than Tanner!

Grabbing a granola bar from the vending machine near the motel office, I tried not to think about my angel's new color. I needed to eat if I was going to hunt. I had to push the thought of maroon angels out of my mind and just be grateful it wasn't black.

After I ate and grabbed a water, I was back on the streets looking for Rosa or Masters or anyone really. At this point, everyone was a suspect. Any person I encountered could be possessed or damned or at the very least, being influenced. It wasn't the best scenario for demon hunting, but it was going to have to work.

I walked the neighborhood but saw nothing. It was about noon when I saw the familiar black Buick driving down the street, and my stomach sank.

"Ugh, that man!" I stood on the corner with my hands on my hips.

Tanner pulled over and rolled down the window.

"Need a ride?" His dimpled smile melted my façade, and I had to grin. It was great to see him, although I'd never tell him that. I got into the car and welcomed the air conditioning. "Any luck out here?" he asked as we drove.

"Not yet, I—" I trailed off as I watched the

streets. "How did you find me?" I asked.

"Wasn't hard. It's a small area, and I just drove up and down every street."

"Wow…" I looked over at him.

He shrugged.

"Stalk much?"

"If you hadn't hung up on me, I wouldn't have to stalk, as you call it. I call it tracking."

"You call it whatever you want." I watched for demonic activity out the window with a slight grin on my face.

We drove past the motel and diner, and I swear I saw what looked like a large black-wing flip around the side of the motel.

"What was that?" I pointed.

"What?" Tanner looked to where I was pointing. There was nothing there, not a soul.

"Nothing," I sighed. "I must be getting tired." I sat and prayed for a moment, not realizing I was praying in tongues.

"What was that?" Tanner asked. "Some weird language?"

"Oh nothing," I lied. "Just a little prayer for safety."

"Good thinking. You have any other superpowers we could use?" he asked.

My eyes widened, and I let out a nervous laugh.

"Ha ha. Superpowers, that's funny." I stammered. "What? Those aren't real." I was suddenly aware that Tanner knew nothing of my power of prayer—my glowing hands. I bit my lower lip. "We should probably have a conversation; I have told you a little about the demons, but there is more," I began.

*　　　*　　　*

Since I hadn't seen any of the people I was looking for on my search by foot or once Tanner had picked me up, we decided to head to the white house while I spilled my guts. Besides, I needed to destroy the small box and the objects inside of it at the house, following the instructions on the paper that Father Kauna gave me to get rid of the curse.

Once I had finished my story, I watched Tanner closely. I had just unloaded five years of my history in the short drive—all of it, St. Michael's Institute of Exorcism and Spiritual Warfare, my specialized training, the charismatic gifts, and my supernatural power of prayer. I left out the glowing hands, for the moment. I needed to gauge his reaction to the easy stuff first.

"Okay, so you're telling me there's a secret part of the Catholic Church, training normal people to go around and banish demons?"

"Something like that, yes."

"Why aren't the priests doing it?"

"That's a great question. First, there aren't

enough of them; and second, they're already working. Those of us that have been trained are special in some way or another."

"What does that mean?" He looked me up and down.

"It's hard to understand. I just know stuff and can do stuff other people can't." I tried to skirt around the subject; but as an FBI agent, he knew how to get the information he wanted. Luckily, we pulled up to the white stucco house.

"We are here," I said and noticed someone boarded up the stained glass window I'd thrown Rosa through. "Will you stay here? In the car?" I asked as I unbuckled my seatbelt.

"Not a chance in hell."

"That's what I figured."

SEVENTEEN

We walked up the staircase to the large, wooden doors. I noticed no one was around; it was too still.

"Let me do what I do…" I said to Tanner, looking into his eyes.

"I will try; but if it gets out of hand in any way, I'm taking over." He patted his holstered gun.

I knew the gun wasn't going to help in this fight, but I let him think he had some power over the situation.

Opening the door slowly, I peered inside; Tanner suddenly pushed past me, pulled his gun, and flew into the house. In a crouched position, he pointed the gun right and left with great speed. I threw my hands in the air.

"What are you doing?"

"My job!" he snapped back.

I rolled my eyes and walked past him.

Tanner was on high alert, flinging his gun around each corner and pushing me aside so he could go first. I followed behind, shaking my head. I knew his gun was useless against the demon; you can't kill evil.

We searched the house but didn't find anyone. I didn't feel the demonic presence strong enough to be in the house; it was certainly near, but not in the house — yet.

Although I had explained my supernatural powers to Tanner, I knew someone in his position wouldn't be able to understand what I was going to do next. I needed him out of the house, so I could perform the cleansing procedure and draw Rosa out of hiding.

"Why don't you go look around the outside of the house?" I said as Tanner paced the foyer.

He nodded and left out the front doors. The door shut behind him; I took the stairs two by two. At the top, I took a right to the room I had found Tanner and the box. I pulled the Padre Pio procedure instructions, the box, and the Padre Pio relic out of my shoulder bag. I looked around for a good place to burn the box. Wood floors were not an option; the wood desk was a no. Searching for a bucket or some container, I mentally kicked myself for not thinking this all the way through before I got here. But then, the door to the bathroom caught my eye.

"Yes!" I said and ran into the bathroom. It was dirty and small, but it would work. A cast iron tub sat in the corner; I knelt on the side of it and put the box in the center of the tub. I pulled out some butane lighter fluid I had bought at a gas station on the way back from the Diocese. Spraying the box, inside and out with butane, I took out a small red lighter and flicked it on. The tiny flame ignited the box in a swoosh of flames; I leaned backwards dodging the fire. It settled quickly, and I peered over the tub to watch the hair shrivel up into nothing, the stench of burnt hair filled the tiny room. The paper was next to burn; its red embers flew around the box. The box itself didn't seem to light; I poured more butane on it.

"What are you doing?" Tanner stood in the doorway, staring at me crouched next to the tub with a burning box inside. I was sure this was a scene his FBI mind would never think he would see.

"Oh, hi," I said and sat up, watching the box to make sure it was on fire. "This is the cursed box. I am burning it."

"With everything you have told me today, this actually makes sense to me," he said and ran his hands through his dark hair. "I don't even know who I am anymore," he whispered and walked out of the bathroom.

"It'll be done in a few minutes," I yelled from the bathroom.

I took the paper Father Kauna gave me and began the procedure prayers. I blessed the burning box with holy water and prayed,

"Father in heaven, we ask you to bind and cast away from us and Rosa and all those who have come into contact with these materials any demonic entities that may have been attached to these materials. We plead in the blood of Jesus over these materials and take back any ground the Evil One may have snatched from us because of the presence of these materials in our possession. Strengthen, O Lord, the hedge of protection around each of us and Rosa. Bless us and Rosa, O Lord. Help us to love you more. We also ask that you be with Rosa and free her from any bondage. Help them to understand Your ways and bless them. We ask these things with the intercession of the Blessed Virgin Mary, Mother of God, Blessed Apostles Peter and Paul, Blessed St. Michael the Archangel, Saints Bruno, Basil, Benedict, and Padre Pio, our guardian angels, and all the saints and angels of Heaven, and powerful in the holy and mighty name of Your Son, Jesus Christ, whose name causes Hell to tremble. Amen."

I sat for a moment as I ended the prayer, looking around the room and watching the box burn. I wasn't sure what would happen next; I knew burning this box would antagonize the demon in Rosa, but I had no idea what it would do to the others in her web of the damned.

A loud bang sounded from the hall. I jumped up and peered out of the bathroom doorway. "Tanner?" I called out. No answer. Before walking out of the bathroom, I checked the burning box once more; it was almost all the way charred. Leaving the box, I searched the room, but it was empty. I walked slowly. The air in the house seemed stale, and the smell of sulfur emanated from the hallway. Someone or something was close.

"Well, hello!" Officer Masters appeared in the doorway, a hand on each side of the frame. Her eyes were a solid black.

"Julie?" I was taken back. "Where is Tanner?" I asked quickly.

"Oh, him? He's busy." Masters strolled into the room like a lion circling its prey.

"What do you want, Officer?"

She looked terrible; her skin was a gray color, dark circles under her eyes, and her clothes were dirty and torn. She looked as if she had just crawled out of the gutter.

"What do you think?" She cocked her head to

the side. "The master has promised great treasure for your death. I intend on cashing in on that promise."

My stomach tightened. I hoped by master she meant Rosa and not the big ole master.

"Treasure? What treasure?"

"To kill the Deliverer would give me great power, more power than master. I want that power." Her eyes narrowed as she took a step toward me.

"Well, you will fail; they all do." I rubbed my hands together. "No one can defeat the power of Christ."

"I know, but you are not the Christ. You are human, and humans are easy."

"You underestimate me." I slipped my hand into my shoulder bag and grabbed the holy water container. "I will give you one chance, demon. Exit this woman now."

It laughed a deep guttural laugh, the kind of laugh an animal would make. I took that as a no and pulled out the holy water, spraying it across the room and hitting Officer Masters with water. She screamed and fell to the floor. I took my chance and jumped on top of her. Straddling her and pinning her arms with my knees, I began to pray. The wisps of light formed on my palms and extended out toward my fingertips. Grabbing her face, I prayed the Prayer of St. Michael and a Hail

Mary; the whole time Masters thrashed and twisted. I held her with my eyes clenched shut and prayed; I saw in my mind the healing glow of God; the beauty and peacefulness of Heaven came into sight. The light filled my view and body with healing light. I felt the power of the Spirit flow through every inch of skin.

Suddenly, the light exploded outward, and Masters slammed against the wooden floor. I fell off to the right.

I felt arms around me, pulling me up to a sitting position.

"Lavive, Lavive, are you okay?" Tanner asked and held me tight.

"What?" My mind was spinning. "Masters?"

"She's right there. I think you knocked her out or something. She's breathing."

"I didn't." I sat up and held my head. "I didn't do that; it was done through me. There is a difference." I blinked wildly; my bearings were coming back quickly. "Are you okay?" I asked Tanner.

"Yes, she got the jump on me and hit me over the head; I will have a bump, but I'm ok."

I turned toward Masters; she looked like herself again. Her skin was pink, and the gauntly gray had gone. The dark circles disappeared, and rosy cheeks appeared. I leaned over her, and taking my thumb and pointer finger, I opened her eyelid. I exhaled; her eyes were back to a pretty brown—much better than the black-oil-slicked eyes of the damned. She was still dirty and disheveled, but I could tell in her face she was free. I didn't need her confirmation; I could feel it.

She stirred. "It's going to be all right." I said to Masters. "You are free."

She opened her eyes, blinking wildly.

"How are you feeling?" I asked.

"My head is killing me. Where am I?" she asked and put her hand against the side of her head. "Who are you?" A confused look settled on her face.

I was grateful she didn't remember, but she couldn't help me find Rosa if she didn't remember anything.

"I'm Agent Tanner O'Connely, FBI." He interjected and showed Masters his badge. "You are safe." That put her at ease, a little. *Having an FBI agent wasn't all bad*, I thought.

Tanner and I got Masters down the stairs and into his car. She didn't remember tricking Tanner or drugging him. We didn't go into details of what she did while possessed. I'd learned over the years, it's better for them that they didn't remember.

"I will take her to the hospital."

"Great, I'll stay here. I need to bury the ashes of the box."

"Oh no! You're not staying here alone."

"Give the tough guy act a rest, Tanner! You saw me. I can handle myself."

His eyes pulled together. "Yes, I saw. You can." He took a breath. "But I want you to stay safe; so just come with me, it'll be fast."

"No," I said and put my hands on my hips. "That is final." I turned and walked back toward the house.

"You are impossible, Lavive Willot!" Tanner yelled from the car. "I will be back in less than thirty minutes. Try to stay out of trouble."

"I'll try." I waved goodbye as he drove away. I took a deep breath and looked up at the setting sun. I needed to get the ashes buried before sunset, but I was tired as it was. Banishing demons back to Hell was a tough job, and I knew I needed all my strength for Rosa. I looked up at the three-story stucco house and settled my gaze on the bedroom window.

"Shit," I whispered as she ducked out of sight.

EIGHTEEN

I had recognized the red dress; it was definitely Rosa. I prayed a St. Michael prayer and headed up the stairs to the house. I had to finish the Padre Pio procedure to destroy the cursed box; I still needed to bury the ashes to finalize the breaking of the curse on Rosa. I carefully, but quickly, climbed the massive stairs, watching out for any sign of Rosa. This tricky demon would do anything to stop me, which was obvious since it had put a bounty on my head. If it was willing to promise immense power, it was willing to do anything.

Opening the door to the room, I carefully scanned the area for Rosa. Taking a quick mental and emotional inventory, I didn't feel her essence. I burst through the door and ran quickly to the bathroom, closing the bathroom door behind me. Like a door would keep out a demon, but some human habits were hard to break. The box in the tub was completely ashes, no sign of embers left. I pulled out a small jar I had in my cross-body bag and scooped up all the ashes I could. The Padre Pio papers said burying was best, but a stream would work too. I looked at the few remnants of ashes in the tub. Not wanting to do anything wrong, I cupped a handful of water from the sink and threw it in the tub. One after another until the ashes went down the drain. It wasn't a stream, but the septic system of Phoenix would have to work.

Putting the small jar of ashes in my bag, I headed out of the bathroom, still on high alert for Rosa. She wasn't in the room; I walked slowly toward the door. The creaking of the floorboards seemed to echo throughout the house. Making it to the stairs, I saw the front door was open, and I hadn't left it open.

"Hello, little Deliverer." A man's voice came from across the hall. He stepped out of a room into view. It was Mitchell from the night before. His eyes were now completely black.

"Oh, you again! What, is Rosa scared to face me herself?"

"Master is not afraid!" he growled. "I asked for the opportunity to get the bounty." His wicked smile told me I needed to get my power flowing, and fast. My palms itched, as I prayed a prayer of protection in my mind. I knew he was a distraction in order to keep me from finishing the procedure to destroy the curse. My angel manifested behind the man; my heart leapt in my chest. He was bright blue with no pink or maroon in sight. Maybe I wouldn't die today.

"Well," I said to Mitchell, "you will have to wait your turn." With that, I threw holy water and blessed oil on him and ran down the stairs. I didn't look back as he hollered in pain. Taking the stairs in epic fashion, I landed on the foyer floor with a thud. I headed for the front door. It slammed shut right as I was about to make my exit. I turned around to see Rosa at the top of the stairs, her hand extended outward controlling the door.

I looked back to the door; my hand wrapped around the doorknob, and I pulled with all my might. It didn't budge. I kept an eye on Rosa who still stood at the top of the stairs with Mitchell at her feet.

I watched Rosa lift her hand over Mitchell, and black smoke seeped from her fingertips. It ran down and encircled Mitchell in a black blanket of evil. She clenched her fist, and the smoke was cut off. Mitchell continued to lie on the floor, twisting and turning in the smoke. I wondered what she was doing to him, but I had to push that aside for the moment.

The front door wasn't going to be my exit to get outside and bury the box. I saw a few sun rays coming from the kitchen. Taking off in a full run, I headed for the back door. I could hear someone barreling down the steps, and I kept running.

Opening the back door, I jumped across the four steps and hit the earth, falling to my knees and rolling. Scrambling to get my bearings, I pulled out my blessed salts and sprinkled them across the threshold of the doorway. It wouldn't stop her, but it would slow her down. I searched for a tool, something to dig with. A one-foot long, four-inch wide piece of wood lay against the chain-length fence. Grabbing the wood, I thrust it into the ground.

At first only, I only made a dent in the hard soil. But I kept hitting the ground, digging more and more and looking up every few moments to the back door, waiting for Rosa. Finally hitting soft soil, I was making headway in the dirt, digging about six inches down. Tossing the wood aside, I pulled the jar with the ashes out of my bag and threw it in the hole.

A scream came from inside the house. I pulled out the Padre Pio prayers and holy water. Sprinkling the jar and saying an Our Father and three Hail Marys, I pushed the earth over the jar, covering it and sealing the area with oil.

Sweat ran down my back; my hands and knees were covered with dirt. Another scream came from the house. Standing, I dusted off my hands and anointed myself with blessed oils before beginning the prayer to remove the attachment to Rosa.

"In the name of the Lord Jesus Christ, strengthened by the intercession of the Blessed Virgin Mary, Mother of God, of Blessed Michael the Archangel, of the Blessed Apostles Peter and Paul, my guardian angel."

He was glowing a bright blue. My hands began to glow as bright as my angel. I took the stairs up into the kitchen and continued the prayer.

"And all the saints, and powerful in the holy authority of His Precious and Wonderful Name, I ask, O Lord God, that you break and dissolve any and all curses, hexes, spells, seals, satanic vows, and pacts."

"Ahhhhhhhh!" Rosa ran at me, tackling me to the kitchen floor.

I wiggled my arms up and pushed my hands against her face. It contorted under my hands; her eye peeked out between my fingers, and it was solid black. The power of the spirit flowed through me, and Rosa pulled away. Able to flip her over, I held her face and continued.

"Spiritual bonding and soul ties with satanic forces, evil wishes, evil desires, hereditary seals, snares, traps, lies, obstacles, deceptions, diversions, spiritual influences, and every dysfunction and disease from any source whatsoever, that have been placed upon Rosa, Father in Heaven. Please rebuke these evil spirits and their effects and cast them away from Rosa, so that she may continue to do Your will and fulfill the mission You have for her to Your Greater Glory."

Rosa bucked under me. I pressed harder against her and pulled my knees up in order to pin her shoulders. She bucked again, and I lost my balance, falling to the right and hitting the kitchen cabinets with my shoulder.

She flew upright and stood over me, a grimace across her face. She didn't look like the beautiful Rosa anymore. She was evil, pure evil.

"You, stupid, little bitch!" she growled. "I will enjoy breaking your spirit!" She grabbed me by the shoulders and with inhuman strength, threw me across the kitchen.

I slammed into the adjacent wall and tumbled to the floor. My entire body exploded with pain. I moaned, as I tried to pick myself up. She was at me before I could stand.

Rosa grabbed my shirt and threw me against the wall, pinning me, with her hands at my throat.

Clawing at her hands, I struggled to breathe.

"See, you little nothing. I am more powerful than you will ever be." She tightened her grip on my neck. "Give up?"

I tried to speak and could only mouth the word no. She dropped me to the ground, and I crumpled like a rag doll. "You are so infuriating! I have been ahead of you at every turn, and you still fight me?" Rosa paused and looked at her black nails. "I bet you would make a great minion," she said to herself. "How about that Deliverer? You work for me?" She smiled, her black stare penetrating my soul.

"I will always fight you, demon, until the day I die!"

"Well, we can arrange that!" she growled and grabbed my leg, pulling me through the kitchen and down the hall, slamming me against the front door in the foyer.

I laid on the floor for a moment; pain rocked through my body. She had super-human strength; I was just a one-hundred-twenty-pound girl. I was getting my ass kicked. I prayed a prayer of strength.

Reaching for my bag, I fumbled getting the flap open.

Rosa kicked the bag and broke the strap off; the bag skidded across the floor. I watched it with dread filling my chest. I needed my tools.

"What will you do now?" Rosa knelt, her face inches from mine.

I saw my refection in her black eyes. I was cradled on the floor, clutching my knees to my chest. I had never felt so weak.

I closed my eyes and began to pray as hard as I had ever prayed in my life. I prayed to the trinity, my angel, all the saints, and especially St. Michael the Archangel. I needed all their intercession to find the strength to fight this demon.

The more I prayed, the hotter my hands grew. I looked down and saw they were burning bright white. The typical wisps of light were thickened and vibrant. The light began at my palms and quickly traveled up my fingers and to my wrists. I watched the light crawl up my forearms and reach my elbows.

Rosa gasped, as she noticed the glow that grew across my skin.

NINETEEN

I felt the power of the Heavens grow as it illuminated my skin. The light covered my arms, up to my shoulders, and spread across my chest. I felt my face heat up. Power surged through me, and I was renewed. The pain had disappeared; I felt strong. I stood slowly as the light covered the rest of my skin.

I extended my arms and prayed in tongues the prayer of deliverance and Rite of Exorcism. Rosa fell to her knees; a loud growl escaped from her. I went toward Rosa, and with each step, she cried out in pain. I wasn't touching her, but the light that I reflected was fighting the demon inside her. I grabbed my bag and pulled out the relic of Padre

Pio; it shown bright in my palm.

Rosa was lying on her side in the fetal position when I got to her. I crouched down and looked her in the eyes. "What will you do now?" I asked in a snarky tone. I may be filled with heavenly light, but I was still human.

I pushed Rosa to her back and put the relic of Padre Pio on her chest, right below her neck. Her body seemed to pull away from the relic and a long hiss escaped her lips. As if frozen under the weight of the tiny relic, she pressed against the floor. I placed my hands on each side of her face, turning it to look into my eyes.

"Rosa! Rosa! I know you are in there. Fight this."

I closed my eyes and lifted my head to the Heavens, praying the Rite of Exorcism. I felt the Holy Spirit pour into Rosa. A sound like a child's cry came from her mouth.

"Please stop. It's killing me," Rosa said softly.

"Demon, you have no power here; your curse is broken, and you will release Rosa, in the name of Jesus Christ."

Rosa sucked in air through gritted teeth. "What is your name, demon?"

Her neck twisted, and her head pressed hard to the left. Her mouth hung open as a low moan escaped. I pressed the relic against her bare skin, and she let out a cry, arching her head back. "Tell me your name!"

"Deliverer, you will not succeed. You will not win this war." A man's voice came from Rosa's lips. "We watch and know all. You and the man will die."

I immediately thought of Tanner. "You have no power here. You have been defeated, and it is now time for you to go back to Hell and to never enter this woman again!" I demanded as I blessed her forehead, lips, and chest with oil. "By the power of our Lord, you will tell me your name."

Light from my hands burst into Rosa's chest. Her body jerked, as the bolt of energy crashed into her.

"A...ce...di...a," the demon said in a long, drawn-out, loud whisper. Acedia, the Noonday Devil. A powerful demon who had been associated with sloth and most recently drugs and addiction. My mind spun; it made total sense that this was the Acedia demon, the demon of procrastination, the demon that withheld all from what they were meant to be. The drug addict was the perfect vessel for Acedia.

"Fight against the demon Acedia; fight against the demons' pull toward the easy. Push with God's love into the light that you are meant to be."

Rosa twisted her body; a ribbon of thick, black smoke came from her mouth. Keeping my hands in front of me, I continued to pray, as I watched the ribbon grow in thickness and length. It wound in a tornado of blackness while pouring out of Rosa's body. I scrutinized it carefully, never ceasing in prayer. It began to take form. Grabbing the holy water, I threw water it.

"Blessed be Jesus Christ, and through Him, I cast you out, the Acedia demon."

The form manifested into a large face that let out a high-pitched scream, and I covered my ears. As the mouth expanded, it opened wide and swallowed the rest of the face, over and over until it had completely engulfed itself.

I sat up, my breathing labored, sweat dripping from my brow. The light that covered my body slowly began to disappear, starting with my legs and moving up. The last lit were my hands. Exhaustion overtook me in that moment; the days of hunting and fighting all hit me. I leaned down against Rosa.

The air was filled with the scent of roses, and I knew it was over. I cradled Rosa's head in my lap.

"Lavive!" I heard Tanner yell from the front door.

"Here." I was able to get out.

Tanner opened the door and fell to the floor, wrapping his arms around me. I leaned against him, my eyes fighting to stay open. I was exhausted.

"What happened?"

"It's over," I said and put my head against his

chest.

I prayed, "Thank you, Father, for hearing my prayer. I praise your Holy Name and worship You and love You. Thank You for the wisdom and light of Your Holy Spirit. Thank You for enabling me through Your Holy Spirit to be aggressive against the works of the enemy. Thank You for Your Hope, which takes away discouragement; thank You for ongoing victory." I blessed Rosa with oil.

Rosa began to stir. "¿Qué ésta pasando? What is happening?" she asked as her eyes blinked open. "Where am I?"

"Rosa, you are safe. I am Lavive, and this is Special Agent O'Connely."

Rosa sat up and held her head. Her skin, although covered with sweat, returned to its fresh tone of light brown. Her eyes were back to the big brown eyes I had seen on that first night I met her in the diner.

"Oh mi, my head is pounding," she said in her lovely Mexican accent.

My heart soared, hearing her again and no remnants of the demon, Acedia. Tanner handed her his handkerchief. She nodded a thanks and blotted her forehead.

"Do you remember anything?"

"No, no. The last thing I remember is the diner; I was working."

Tanner and I helped her to her feet, and we all

stood in the abandoned house. Although dark and dirty it was the most beautiful house I had ever seen. Rosa seemed to glow with the Holy Spirit, and for the first time, her angel appeared to me.

It manifested alongside Rosa and extended its wing around her. It shown a beautiful blue. I observed him watching her. I didn't know where it had been or why I hadn't seen it all this time, but I assumed the demon was so powerful it overshadowed or pushed out the good. There were so many questions; each case I learned a little more about the spiritual warfare and myself.

"Señorita!" Rosa looked at me. "I remember you from the diner. What is going on here?" she asked.

I questioned whether to tell her the truth. Knowing it was a curse that was put on her by someone she would have known, I thought it better if I did tell her. I hoped she was ready to hear this crazy story.

"Let's get out of here, and I will tell you everything," I said and wrapped my arm in hers.

TWENTY

After the short drive and long talk, Rosa was completely up to speed on what had transpired over the past few days.

"I … I can't believe I did any of that," she said with tears in her eyes.

"It wasn't you; you must not blame yourself."

"So many people died. How will I ever … forgive … forget?" She looked at me; her eyes were drawn together, the pain written all over her face.

"My advice is to go to Mass daily, go to Confession, and pray. All these things will help bring some solace. There is a great priest in the Diocese of Phoenix I would like you to see. He is aware of your situation, and I know can help you

through this difficult period." I gave her Father
Kauna's card. I blessed her with holy oil and water
and gave her some to bless the perimeter of her
house and all the windows and doors. Whoever
put a curse on her, hadn't been found, so she
needed to be vigilant against the Evil One and
protect herself and the ones she loved.

"Do you have any idea who would have put a
curse on you?" I asked Rosa.

"I don't know who it was; I don't know many
people here. I have only lived in the area for six
months; before that, I was in Guadalajara, Mexico."

"Do you think it was someone in Mexico?
Someone with Kenyan ties."

"Kenya?" she asked and looked off into the
distance.

"Yes, the curse originates from a tribe in
Kenya."

"Si, Si," she said and paced outside her house. "I
know someone from Kenya. He was a friend of
mine when I first got to America; he came from a
province in Kenya. I think the Nyanza Province."

"Do you think he could have cursed you?"

She looked at me and winked. "He liked me,
although I did not have the same feelings for him."

"Ah," I said. "Makes sense. He loved, and you
didn't love him back; he cursed you in retaliation."

"I don't know if he would do such a thing?"
Rosa said. "He is a very good man."

"Even the best people can make terrible mistakes. Most of the time the people who do the curses have no idea what they are doing and can end up really hurting the people they care the most for," I explained. "You will be okay if you do all of these things I suggested. Remember, where there is God, the Devil cannot enter."

"Gracias, señorita." She wrapped me in a tight hug.

"You are very welcome." I watched her as she walked up to her small, blue house. There weren't any strange feelings or bad vibes I got off the premises. It seemed the demon had completely left her. I exhaled loudly.

"Are you okay, Lavive?" Tanner wrapped an arm around my waist.

"Yes, just tired, it's exhausting kicking demon ass." I smiled, and Tanner laughed.

"I bet it is!"

"How is Officer Masters?"

"She is confused, but overall doing well." Tanner pulled me toward the passenger side of his car. "Let's go."

I couldn't agree more.

We drove to the motel in silence. I was running through the day and night, the past week in Phoenix, the possession and freedom of Rosa, and then there was Tanner. He was an unexpected asset. I hadn't ever imagined myself with someone,

especially someone like him. I looked over at him
as he drove us. He was handsome—that wasn't up
for debate—but what else? He was tough,
thoughtful, and overly protective. All of which
annoyed me, yet I reluctantly found comforting. He
looked over at me.

"What?" he asked. "You are staring at me"

"Just thinking," I said and turned away.

He reached over and squeezed my knee.
"Sometimes you think too much."

"Ha! Look who's talking!" I laughed.

"Yeah, maybe you're right."

"I usually am." I said and gave him a slight grin.
He shook his head and fought a smile.

We pulled up to the motel and parked. Sitting in
the still of the night, neither of us reached for the
door handles.

"I will walk you in." Tanner broke the silence
and opened his door.

I sat while he circled the car to my door. He
opened it and put his hand out for me to take. I
looked at it and then at him, his smile was sultry. I
shook my head and took his hand. He pulled me
out of the car and into his arms. "What is it about
you?" he asked and kissed me gently on the mouth.
I wrapped my arms around his neck and deepened
our kiss. I was tired, but not that tired.

We walked slowly to the door of the motel
room. I stopped at the door and spun around to

face him. "I want you to come in," I said with the sexiest voice I could muster.

His eyes widened. "Are you sure?"

"Yes." I was sure, I was so sure.

I opened the door and flipped on the lights. I felt the scream before I heard it. Jumping back, I fell right into Tanner. We stumbled in the doorway.

"What are you doing here?" I asked Mitchell, his gun pointing straight at my heart. His eyes black as coal. I heard Tanner suck in a breath. "It's fine; it's all fine." I put my hands up and took a couple steps inside the room.

"Lavive!" Tanner yelled.

I didn't look back. I began to pray in my mind and heart. I knew I could defeat a damned, but I wasn't able to dodge a bullet. My hands began to warm.

"It's ok. Look at me," I said, trying to calm the situation.

"You took the master! You took the master," he said over and over.

"I know you're confused; I understand."

"You understand nothing, Deliverer!" He growled.

I saw Tanner take a stance out of the corner of my eye. Staying in-between Tanner and Mitchell, I needed to make sure Tanner didn't kill this guy, even though he had all the legal rights.

"What is your name?

"My name is not important. You took master; I am alone. That is who I am — Alone!"

"You are not alone, I promise. It may seem that way right now, but there is a better way. Come with me, and I can show you." I reached out my hand.

He flinched and lifted the gun to my head. I couldn't breathe.

"You did this," he said as saliva dripped from the corner of his mouth. "You took everything. Now, I will take everything from you." He pointed the gun at Tanner.

"No!" I yelled and jumped in front of the gun. "You want me, not him. This is between us."

"Lavive!" Tanner yelled again.

I waved him off. I took a few more steps toward Mitchell.

"We can figure this out together." My hands began to glow, as the wisps of light darted from my palms. I felt the Holy Spirit flow through me.

Mitchell dodged the wisps of light, waving them off like you would shoo a fly.

"You are loved. You matter," I said as more light flowed from my palms.

The light flew out in strands that wrapped around Mitchell. He fought the light and tried to wave it off. I took my opportunity and jumped forward, tackling him against the bed. Tanner was at my side with the speed of a cheetah, grabbing the gun, and then pulling his out and pointing it at Mitchell.

"Stop, Tanner. I got this!" I said and straddled Mitchell, pressing my hands against his cheeks. I prayed in angelic tongues, and the power flowed from me into him. He arched his back and screamed. I held on and prayed. "Father, I now place my enemies into Your hands. Look with mercy upon them, and do not hold their sins against them. Anyone who has cursed me, I now bless. Anyone who has hurt me, I now forgive. For those who have persecuted me, I now pray." Then, I finished with an Our Father, Hail Mary, and the Glory Be.

Mitchell calmed enough that I was able to grab the blessed oil from my cross-body bag and bless his forehead, hands, and chest. His eyes closed and body relaxed under me. I knew this demon was the last part of the whole beast, which was Acedia.

I opened Mitchell's mouth and dripped a few drops of holy water on his tongue. The black ribbon of smoke began to form and twirl out of his mouth and up toward the ceiling. I prayed for deliverance and healing, as the ribbon thickened until the tail end of it escaped. It swirled and dissipated into a few black ashes that fell to the ground.

"What the actual Hell, Lavive!" Tanner whispered from behind me.

I looked back and by the look on his face, I knew I would have to explain the glowing hands thing to Tanner. I turned back to Mitchell. He began to stir and opened his eyes. They were a pretty green.

"Hi," I said and smiled.

"Who are you and why are you sitting on me?" he asked.

"Oh, yeah, sorry." I crawled off him. As soon as I was off, Tanner swooped in and threw him on his stomach, holding both hands behind his back. "What are you doing, Tanner?"

"What do you think? This guy just tried to kill both of us; I am arresting his ass!" Tanner cuffed him and pulled him up by his arm. "Come on." He dragged Mitchell out of the room as he read him his Miranda Rights.

TWENTY-ONE

I ran out of the motel room after them; the police were pulling up, sirens blaring. Tanner had Mitchell in the parking lot.

"He didn't know what he was doing, Tanner!" I yelled over the sound of sirens.

"I don't give a shit, Lavive. This is my job!" he yelled back and glared at me.

I took a second to breathe. My hands on my hips, I watched the police exit their vehicles, guns pulled. I rolled my eyes, full knowing Mitchell wasn't a threat. I didn't know what kind of man he was, but I did know he wasn't possessed with any demonic forces anymore. They put him in the back of a police car; he looked at me. I waved and tried to smile even though he was going to jail. No one could threaten an FBI agent and not go to jail.

I sat on the curb of the parking lot, watching Tanner and the other cops talk and take notes. One of them came to take my statement. I told them what I wanted to and left out the bits and pieces of glowing hands and black, demon smoke. I hoped Tanner did the same.

"Hey," Tanner said as he knelt by me. "I'm sorry, Lavive. I didn't mean to yell at you. You have to understand, this is my job. I have to do this."

"And you have to understand that freeing that man from his attachment is my job."

"I saw you; I get it." He put his hands on my cheeks and stared me in the eyes. "I believe you; I believe what you do. I don't know how you do it, why or anything else. I don't even know if I believe in Heaven and Hell. But I believe in you." Tanner's voice was as sincere as I had ever heard him. I placed my hands on his.

"Thank you. I guess that will have to do... for now." I smiled, and he kissed my forehead.

He stood and went back to the group of cops huddled around the cars. I watched for a while; it's funny how I ran from them all this time, and now here, I sit as a witness, a consultant of sorts. I guessed you never really knew where life would lead you. I certainly didn't think it was taking me here. I looked over at my angel who floated to my right. He bent down and extended a wing over me. I leaned toward him, feeling the power of peace he radiated. Looking up at his face, I grinned; and for the first time in my life, he smiled back.

My grin widened and heart leapt in my chest. "Hi!" I said, as if we were just meeting. He didn't say anything; and the smile only lasted a few moments, but it was there—I saw it! I didn't know what it meant, but I was so grateful to have that tiny assurance that he was with me and understood me. All these years he'd been there, but as an observer, always on the outside. I felt for the first time a real human connection with my angel, and it was nothing less than magical. But why was it happening now?

Maybe the body-glow power I had developed from earlier tweaked some charisms I have, and now I could see my angel's expressions? Or it could just be because he thought I had earned a little gift. I didn't know if I would ever really understand the workings of my angel or the demons I hunted, but I did know it's what I was born to do.

"Let's go in." I jumped as Tanner touched my shoulder. "Are you ok?" he asked, his eyes shown concern.

"Yes," I laughed a little. "Yes, I am great." I stood, still looking my angel in the eyes. I smiled and turned away as Tanner wrapped an arm around my waist and began leading me to the motel room.

"I know this night has been — well — crazy! But I need to know you are okay."

"I am fine, Tanner. All this has been a bit intense and not exactly what I am used to, but I can handle it."

"You amaze me," he whispered. I turned around and cupped his cheeks, looking deep into his eyes.

"I am fine, promise." I kissed him softly.

He wrapped his arms around me tight and buried his face in the crook of my neck. "You are very sweet when you want to be." He laughed a little.

"Are you done here?" I asked.

He muttered a yes.

"Let's go inside." I pulled away and took his hand. He followed as I went back into the motel room.

The room was the same as we left it except missing the guy with a gun pointed at my head. I could go a thousand lives without that happening again. I flopped down on the bed, exhaling loudly. Tanner stood at the door watching me.

"What?" I asked.

He shook his head. "Nothing. You are just beautiful."

"Oh, well thank you, Agent." I reached out for

his hand. He took it, and I pulled him to me. We both fell against the bed. He snuggled next to me and pulled me into his arms. I lay there for a minute smelling him and feeling his strong arms surrounding me. I was content.

"I have one question."

"Just one?" I asked. "You watched me cast a demon out of a man, and you only have one question?"

"Well, for now," he said.

"Okay."

"What the hell is this? The land of the freaking damned?"

I couldn't help but laugh. "No, it's just a town with a demon problem, just like hundreds of other towns," I said and snuggled deeper into his arms. "It's never-ending these days. Let's just say, I have job security."

Tanner nodded, but I wasn't sure if he really understood how prolific the demonic influence really was.

I laid on his bicep as his other arm wrapped around my waist. I let myself relax and fall into a peaceful sleep.

*   *   *

Tanner stirred. I had been awake for an hour, but his deep breathing and few snores told me he was still sleeping. As I lay there, I thought of the past week's events. Who knew the FBI agent that followed me from Chicago would be my snuggle partner? I thought of the lives that were lost—Emily, Kevin, Officer Matthews and the many before I came to town. Mad I couldn't be faster or do more, I knew it all worked out the way it was supposed to. God always had a plan, even if I didn't agree with it.

"Hey." Tanner stretched, "How long have you been up?"

"A little while—"

"Sorry." He yawned. "I must have been exhausted!"

"I think we both were, and we deserve some rest."

"Agreed!" He said, staring at the ceiling. We both lay there in silence. I contemplated every step I had taken the past week and only assumed Tanner was doing the same.

"I'm hungry," I said and rolled over, pulling my dreadlocks to the side. "The diner is open; let's get some food."

Tanner leaned toward me and kissed me on the nose. "Sounds good, babe."

I took a quick shower and changed; Tanner had some clothes in his car and was able to freshen up. The sun was rising, making pink and orange streaks across the sky as we walked across the street to the diner. I held my cross-body bag and pulled out the holy water and oil.

"What is that for? I thought we were done?" Tanner asked and pointed toward the bottles in my hand.

"We are, sort of, just need to bless the diner. A lot of action happened there; it's good to seal up all the loose ends," I explained. "There are remnants of Evil that need to be cleaned; you can't see it, but it's there."

He rubbed his stubble chin. "Do what you need to do. I am getting coffee." He yawned.

I laughed and pushed him inside the diner's doors. I stayed back to bless the perimeter of the building. Starting with the front door, I blessed the opening, dripped some holy water, and sprinkled some blessed salts on the threshold. Moving west, I walked the perimeter of the building, praying and sprinkling holy water as I went. Rounding the building, I noticed the back door of the kitchen was propped open. A white plume of steam escaped from the top of the door. I walked closer; the smell of onions stung my senses. The hair on my arms stood on end.

TWENTY-TWO

Her scream pierced my ears. "¡Oh Dios mío! What are you doing lurking back here? You scared me!" Rosa yelled as she pointed a knife at me.

"Rosa, it's me, Lavive." I raised my hands and eyed the knife.

"Oh, sorry!" She lowered the knife. "I was chopping onions and had the door opened to let some air in. I heard something." Rosa laughed and leaned against the back of the building. "I guess that something was you!"

"So sorry, I was just blessing the building." I held up the holy water and oil.

"Oh, please continue. Will you bless me again? You can never have too many blessings."

"Absolutely." Taking some oil, I made the sign of the cross on her forehead and in each palm, praying a healing prayer as I did.

"Thank you," she said with tears in her eyes. "You saved my life yesterday. You brought me back. I had been living in a fog for so long. I didn't know a way out, but you did it!"

"I didn't do it. I was just a vessel for the Holy Spirit. Your will and His love did it."

She hugged me tight. She smelled of onions, like always, but now roses, too.

"Please, come in and sit. Your man is already inside. I will feed you!"

"I will. Just let me finish up here, and I will be in soon."

She nodded and turned to go back inside the restaurant.

"Hello." A man's voice came from the side of the building.

Rosa and I stopped and stared in the direction of the man. The tall, beautiful, black man I had seen in the diner a few times rounded the corner of the building.

"I am Hiuhu," he said to me and turned to Rosa. "I am so sorry, Rosa, I didn't know." His eyes got teary.

"It was you?" I asked.

"Si," Rosa said and crossed her arms. "It was him."

"Yes, it was me. I put the curse on Rosa. I was so heartbroken, and my great aunt had taught me about a small curse for enemies. Obviously, it exploded into something awful."

"You got that right!" I scoffed.

"I have been watching Rosa and keeping her safe when I could. Then you came, and I knew you could help her." He nodded at me.

"I'm not letting you off the hook. You put a curse on someone! That's a huge deal!" I yelled.

"I am so sorry, Rosa. I tried to take it off, to put a counter curse; and I think I made it worse. I will never mess with that magic again. I promise," he explained.

"Fine, if you say that, then you won't mind me blessing you," I said and held up the holy water and oils.

Hiuhu nodded and knelt to his knees. I took the oil and water and blessed him. I didn't feel any evil coming from him; I didn't see any signs of the damned. Maybe he was just a man who had gotten in way over his head. Rosa stood at the back door and watched, her face like stone.

"You need to leave here and never come back," I said to him.

"I will. I'll never return." He looked at Rosa. "I promise." With that, Hiuhu turned and disappeared around the diner.

Rosa had tears running down her face.

"It's really over, Rosa. I promise."

She nodded and wiped her face, then turned

and went back into the kitchen.

Getting back to blessing the building, I put some salt down on the threshold of the back door and some holy water on the perimeter of the rest of the building. After I was satisfied with the blessing, I put the rest of the holy water and oil back in my bag.

Entering the diner, the air seemed lighter. The sun was brighter, and everyone appeared a bit happier. I couldn't help but smile. Once at my table, I found Tanner had already ordered coffee for the two of us.

"Why are you so smiley?" Tanner asked as I sat down.

I shrugged. "Just a good day," I said and took a sip of coffee. Even the coffee tasted better. Well, it wasn't laced with meth, so that helped, of course. Was it possible to have demonic flavored coffee? A laugh escaped my lips.

"What?" Tanner asked

"It's nothing." I waved him off. He'd think I was insane.

"Hola, again!" Rosa said as she bounced over to our table. "What will you have?"

I ordered my usual with extra hash browns. Tanner picked a southwestern omelet, bacon, and a biscuit on the side. He was hungry! We laughed and talked for a while as we waited for our food. I didn't tell him about Hiuhu. I knew Tanner, and he would have overreacted, which seemed to be an appropriate reaction for an FBI agent. But it wasn't what we needed. I had taken care of Hiuhu, and Rosa was safe now.

"Excuse me." I heard another man's voice at our table.

I looked up to see the tall man from the street corner that had been with Officer Masters and Mitchell. I sucked in a breath and rubbed my hands together, saying a quick prayer of strength in my mind. I was about sick of these bad guys showing up!

"Hello," I said and cocked my head to the side.

"I'm Alex. I remember you," he paused and rubbed the back of his neck. "I remember it all. Mitchell didn't know what he was doing, I promise." His eyes were wide, and he bit his bottom lip. "He was under some heavy drugs and some other stuff I can't really explain. I said and did some things, too. I don't know why I did them. It was as if I was inside, looking out, not really being able to control everything, but just enough that I knew what I was doing."

"I completely understand, Alex," I said and reached out for his hand.

He looked at my hand for a moment and eventually took it. "It's all better now."

"It is," he said as tears formed in his eyes, "Although Mitchell is in jail."

I looked over to Tanner and pursed my lips.

"Yes, I know," I said to Alex, as Tanner shrugged and took a gulp of coffee. "Hopefully not too long. You take care of yourself."

"I will. Thank you again." Alex headed toward the door before turning back and waving goodbye.

I waved and kicked Tanner under the table.

"What?" He asked his eyes wide. "I had to arrest the guy. He threatened to kill us both."

"I know," I said reluctantly. "I just don't like it."

As Alex was leaving, Officer Julie Masters walked in the diner. I nodded to Tanner, who looked over his shoulder at her. He stood and took a few strides to meet her in the middle of the room. They shook hands, and I wondered why she didn't get arrested. She did kick me in the chest and kidnap an FBI agent, not to mention help him drug himself. I was already pissed off when they returned to the table.

"Lavive, it's nice to see you again," Masters said.

"I'd say the same." I rubbed my chest under my neck.

"I have been waiting for you two to come to the diner." She scooted in close to me, and I pressed against the window.

"Lavive, I am so sorry about kicking you. I know I have told you before, but I was under some sort of control or something. I didn't even know what I was doing. I mean I did, but I didn't.

Tanner, I am so sorry for kidnapping you and the drugs…" She trailed off. "I have been racking my brain as to how this could have happened to me, and I just don't get it." She lowered her head. "I know you saved me, Lavive." She looked up at me, her eyes full of tears. "Thank you."

I couldn't help it; I knew a normal person wouldn't have done the things she did. "I forgive you," I said and meant it. I wrapped one arm around her. "You're going to be ok." I pulled out a Padre Pio healing and deliverance prayer from my bag. "Read this and do the things listed here. It will help you come to terms with everything that has happened."

She took the paper and thanked me again. "I just wanted to see you one more time, to say thank you from the bottom of my heart; and Agent O'Connely, thank you for not arresting me."

"You are welcome," Tanner said, and I glared at him. Picking and choosing who he arrested really pissed me off. Officer Masters nodded and turned to leave the restaurant. As she walked out the door, I crossed my arms across my chest and pursed my lips. "I know what you're thinking, Lavive!" Tanner said, raising his hands. "I made a call while you were blessing the diner, and they are letting Mitchell go this morning. I'm not pressing charges; he will get probation at most."

I playfully swatted at his hand. "You kept me in

suspense! But thank you!"

We ate our breakfasts, and things seemed for once to just be perfect. I had defeated the demons and got a maybe-boyfriend in the process. Pulling my dreadlocks into a messy bun, I felt good, for the first time in days. I felt good. Then, the phone rang.

Tanner stepped away from the booth to take that call. Another reason not to have a phone, I thought. I watched him talk; his once bright and happy face had fallen into a furrowed brow, and he rubbed his chin. His shoulders slumped over, as he took notes on a tiny pad of paper he'd pulled from his back pocket. As he hung up, he looked at me, concern in his eyes.

"What is it?" I asked when he reached the booth

"Work," he said, sitting down. "I have to leave—today."

"Oh," I sank into the booth. I hadn't thought past this morning. I didn't think he'd leave so soon. "Why and where?" I asked always needing more details.

"Actually," he perked up. "Maybe you can help me with this."

"What do you mean?"

"Well, there have been a rash of murders that started in California and continued in the Las Vegas area."

"Well, Vegas isn't the safest place on earth! It is called Sin City for a reason," I said.

"Right, but these all have one prostitute in common. And law enforcement can't seem to tie her to the murders."

"How can I help? Sounds like a cop's job." I took a sip of coffee.

"The odd thing is how the victims are dying. No one can seem to find any way in or out of the rooms, and they are all healthy men having heart attacks. Plus, one very strange mark is being left on each body. It seems it took them until the third body to notice. But I asked them to send me a picture of the mark."

At that moment, his phone buzzed. He opened the attachment and squinted his eyes. "What do you make of this?" He gave me the phone.

I sucked in a breath and looked back at Tanner. "You need my help."

References

Procedure to Destroy Occultic or Cursed Objects, St. Padre Pio Center for Deliverance Counseling, https://www.saintpiocenter.org

An Exorcist Explains the Demonic, (The Antics of Satan and His Army of Fallen Angels) Fr. Gabriele Amorth with Stefano Stimamiglio, ©2016

His Angels at Our Side, (Understanding Their Power in Our Souls and the World), Fr. John Horgan, © 2018

Order of Blessing of a New Home, Book of Blessings, Bishop's Committee on the Liturgy ©1989

Order for a Blessing to be Used in various Circumstances, Book of Blessings, Bishop's, Committee on the Liturgy © 1989

Catholic Household Blessings and Prayers, Bishop's Committee on the Liturgy, National Conference of Catholic Bishops © 1988

Exorcismus domus a daemonio (exorcism of a house troubled with an evil spirit), Appendix to an edition of the Rituale Romanum, A.D. 1621

Confessions of a
Demon Hunter
~2~

Sign up for the newsletter and learn
more about the upcoming releases at
www.BrandiLeighAuthor.com

Made in the USA
Las Vegas, NV
26 June 2022

50757654R00128